# DOWNHILL

LASZLO KOLLAR

Grosvenor House
Publishing Limited

This book is published by
Grosvenor House Publishing Ltd
Link House
140 The Broadway, Tolworth, Surrey, KT6 7HT.
www.grosvenorhousepublishing.co.uk

This book is a work of fiction. Any resemblance to
people or events, past or present, is purely coincidental.

A CIP record for this book
is available from the British Library

ISBN 978-1-80381-759-0
eBook ISBN 978-1-80381-760-6

I would like to say thank you to Jetta, Zsofia, Szabolcs, and Krisztian, friends of mine who also accepted the role of test reader.

Also, I owe a massive thank you to Robert Kuykendall for the excellent photo that I utilized for the cover design and, last but not least, my editor, Kathie Weaver.

# Chapter 1

The edge of the kitchen counter was slowly getting covered with tiny shards of ice. Sam was getting more and more pissed by the minute, and his wife's sarcastic words echoing in his head didn't help. *"I can't believe how clumsy you are, honey, seriously!"* When he finally managed to crack and chisel out four truncated blocks of ice, he threw them into a glass and flooded them with a double gin, almost a triple. Despite being a gin and tonic guy, Sam didn't make a big deal out of lacking the latter one. He had a big, fat gulp of straight gin and walked back to his home office, eased by the thought that whatever mess he had left in the kitchen would melt anyway.

*"Hey man, you're back? What took you so long?"*

"Nothing, just the ice gave me a bit of a hard time."

*"Hard time how?"*

"Popping the cubes out of these shitty trays is a pain in the ass."

*"Ah. I thought you been waiting for the water to freeze."*

"Piss off!"

Reception this far from town and in the hills was not the strongest. Hence, the quality of the video call was more like Sam's high school exit exam in history—a soft-hearted C-. He's always had better sense of numbers and figures, than dates and events. But Dylan needed Sam's assistance to rectify a rejected application for a project fund. Not a typical emergency, but Sam's dense daily schedule and the closeness of the deadline made it urgent. Before getting home, Sam had phoned Dylan to tell him to prepare the papers, emails, and everything else they needed to get it done tonight. It took them about an hour to finish it. But it wasn't the poor internet signal to blame for this length, neither was the amount of work required. Some of this time was spent with having a little fun, like suggesting obscene pictures as attachments, a rather enthusiastic analysis of the daily sports results despite their lack of expertise, and even a negotiation over Sam's fee. For the latter one, tonic surprisingly wasn't offered nor requested despite its absence.

*"Okay then, talk later. And thanks again!"*

"Yeah, yeah, fine, bye, goodnight!"

Sam hit the end call icon, grabbed his glass, and stood up, stretching his parts a bit.

Samuel Hayes owned several properties, including a penthouse downtown, a humble beach house, and a few others spread across the state. Most people wouldn't pick this house as a first choice, yet this was the place Sam most preferred to spend his free time. Even the not so free. For him, this was the room to carry out the part of his job that required him to sit at a desk in front of a computer. He could never really tell why he liked it so much. It would've been convenient to blame his countryside childhood for his close to none liking of big city life. But he believed that, no matter where you grew up, at some point you'll desire to live in a quieter, more spacious place. Sam, however, didn't choose farming to make his living, so keeping cities out of his life entirely wasn't really an option. But whenever he could, he stayed away from the concrete jungle.

He had no problem with concrete itself, as the unique style of this house clearly demonstrated. Rather, it was the noise, the rush, and mostly the crowd since you didn't get to choose who was in it. This was the reason he considered this house, especially this room, his headquarters. He called this room his workroom when he had to refer to it from time to time, but it was more like a combination study, bedroom, and gym. In the middle, there was a workstation made up of a walnut desk and a dark-grey swivel chair.

After his brief stretch and a few paces, Sam felt the blood starting to flow back to the numb parts of his body. Given that he was 6'2" and had a relatively thick physique, his body parts had huge distances between them, so his blood had quite a task bringing the life back to his entire body. Sam stood by his desk, enjoying the view and the calm, as he waited for the numbness to subside. It was quiet except for the hissing of the rising wind outside, the buzzing of a case fan bearing in the laptop, and the clinking of keys in a pocket of Sam's pants.

Even when he was calm, Sam occupied his free hands with the contents of his pockets, an old habit from his school years. Keys and coins endured the treatment, unlike the poor tissues, receipts, and old parking tickets, which tended to suffer major damage when Sam wasn't so calm. Once, Sam's wife, Lindsey, had called him out about the trash hiding in his pockets when she had discovered some before washing his pants. Sam had delivered a rather pointed reply: *"At least I'm not popping my fingers until they're numb or chewing my fingers until they bleed."* Lindsey never raised her voice about this issue again.

While Sam's left hand was molesting his keys, his right hand was stirring the last sip of diluted gin and ice. As he brought this mix to his mouth, all of a sudden, a strange noise hit his ear. A small explosion reduced to a louder pop just as a sharp pain ripped into his back, forcing him to fall to the ground between his desk and the sofa. He felt his face smash against the floor. The lights shut down and the noises stopped.

# Chapter 2

Austin was walking back and forth between the light-gray walls of the corridor. There wasn't much left in his fingers to pop, and you couldn't even light up a smoke in here. Sunken cheeks, eyes filled with red veins from sleepless nights, Austin was tall and lean, but the past few days had slimmed him down even more than battling pneumonia last year.

As the waiting began to feel like an eternity, he spotted a figure in a white coat approaching him. A tall, good-looking man, somewhere in his 50s or 60s. There are certain situations one can't really get used to despite years of practice, and Austin could tell this was one of those for the doctor the minute he stepped up to Austin and began to explain the situation. Austin listened silently and patiently for as long as he could while every fiber of his body protested against the doctor's words.

"What?"

"Believe me, we are doing everything we can . . ."

"You . . . you cannot be serious."

"I'm terribly sorry, sir. There are still numerous tests we need to run to be able to say more. Because, as of this moment, we can't really tell what could cause this. It is very unfortunate. I'm very sorry."

Austin didn't let the doctor go right away, hoping he would say something encouraging. But he didn't. Encouragement only came from his unspoken words. Once the doctor was gone, Austin just kept standing there, helpless. No more walking from wall to wall, no popping his fingers, no craving for smokes, nothing. He had only one thought, and it caused his throat and chest to shrink unbearably tight. The thought weighed terribly on him and nested itself inside his head, leaving no room for anything else.

*My daughter will not walk again?*

# Chapter 3

A pleasantly mild day shifted to an unusually cool night. In the valley, the descending darkness was mingling with last rays of light, but up here, the darkness had nothing to challenge it. And neither did the silence. Regardless of how fierce the battle between day and night, none of them carried anything this far that could supersede the silence. It was always in charge here. The city lights reached this far, but the noises did not. It was a place skirting the mountain ridges, a place where the birds were the primary noise polluters.

The view was breathtaking, whether looking down to the lit city or up to the unclouded, starry sky. But the enchantment of the valley and the sky did not affect Austin. All his attention was concentrated on the concrete house.

A burly myrtle bush hid Austin even though it swayed and flapped in the wind from time to time. His hands were shaking but not from the cold. He never had trouble with the blood flowing through his limbs, so his hands didn't usually shake even without gloves. But now, he was terribly nervous. If he had eaten anything, he'd have thrown it all up by now. Perhaps our body tries to defend us from just that by the lack of appetite.

Austin straightened and started to slowly approach the house. *I could still turn back*, he thought. *As long as I'm not spotted, I could go back.* But he hadn't spent weeks on end contemplating this move and preparing for this very occasion just to beat a retreat in the last minute.

The house itself didn't quite fit into its environment insofar as concrete doesn't fit into nature, and its design defied the usual style for a house built on a steep slope. Instead of a light, elegant structure with thin stilts and giant panoramic windows, this house looked more like a rectangular concrete bunker and had to be buttressed by massive pillars because the soil around it was gone. Where glass panels might usually go, it had gray concrete walls with a couple of windows here and there. The large room in the front was the exception. Nearly its entire front wall, from floor to ceiling and end to end, was made of glass. Beyond that was a narrow balcony. Instead of a handsome glass balustrade separating the balcony from the abyss below, the gray concrete walls continued at railing height.

Although the house was vulnerable to attack for its aesthetics, its layout was indisputably practical. The dimensions, mainly the height, had been designed to accommodate the steepness of the slope, and the result was that the rooftop and the road were level. A bridge connected the rooftop and the road, providing enough parking space for two cars as regulations required, without turning a single cubic yard of concrete into a garage. It was a kind of reverse layout, which made the process of arriving home by car uniquely effortless, especially when it came to houses on steep slopes.

The house was on a narrow road, which continued up the hill beyond it, and the nearest houses were about three-quarters of a mile away. Austin had spent hours on the paths of the forested hillside looking like an ordinary hiker. As a matter of fact, he wasn't really much more than that. Except for the special attention he had paid to the lone, concrete house through his binoculars.

That cool, starry night, Austin thoroughly checked the perimeter before crossing the road and starting to descend the scree slope toward the rear left corner of the house, where the only entrance was located. He moved very carefully so as not to release a piece of loose rock. He didn't want to make any noise just yet. He descended until he reached the top of the retaining wall that held back the soil. The entrance was almost within reach but not the door itself. A small, narrow terrace, just big enough to put shoes out, stuck out from the house there. The terrace railing was easy enough to hop over from the retaining wall. When he did so, Austin saw that the terrace was lit, intensifying the pressure on him. His plan was to make some kind of noise to lure Sam to the door. He thought that a rather ordinary noise would inspire a person to check out the noise without first grabbing a gun or a phone, so Austin had brought a small branch to tap against the glass door.

The door was also accessible in an easier way, and it was more concealed. Alongside the left wall, a stairway led down from the rooftop and was practically hidden from sight behind the second external wall. Austin hadn't even noticed it until he had once spotted Sam walking down from the roof to the door. For Austin, the darkest route was the most ideal, even though he hadn't spotted cameras during his surveys, not by his naked eye nor through the lenses of his binoculars. Still, just to be sure, he quickly scanned the area surrounding the door, checking every little spot he couldn't have seen from farther away. No sign of a surveillance system.

Stepping to the door, Austin raised his gun in front of him, the branch ready in his other hand. First, he slowly tried the doorknob, and to his surprise, the door opened. He paused, listening. Then he leaned over the railing, let the branch fall over onto the scree slope, and carefully slipped inside.

The house was almost entirely dark. There were no lights on except in the large room. A bluish-gray light from the night sky shone through the windows, providing some light in the rooms not lit by lamplight.

Austin found himself in a short, narrow corridor that continued to the left a few steps away. It was like a thin-soled, reverse letter "L," on the stem of which Austin turned after a quick look around. On his left, there were two smaller rooms, one of which seemed to be a bathroom. The wall on the right had a huge arched opening that led to the living room.

Austin focused entirely on the one room at the end of the corridor—the large room that was attached to the balcony. The door was ajar. He heard footsteps and light streamed into the corridor from the doorway. Austin eyeballed the open door and figured out that sticking to the right wall reduced his chances of being spotted through the door opening. Given the angle the door was ajar, he probably got it just about right. Austin moved forward very slowly, staying close against the corridor's right wall. He was determined, but the thought—*It's not too late to turn back*—did cross his mind. He'd taken five or six steps, his heart pounding in his chest, when a beeping sound stopped him in his tracks. *He must be busy doing something*, Austin thought. He took one more step, and then he saw a figure through the door opening. Full-face mask, black outfit, and, in one hand, what looked like a long gun.

Austin stood frozen in place, petrified, only for a few seconds, but long enough to gain a considerable handicap. He started to move backwards along the right wall, the same way he'd come. He barely had about seven more feet to reach the end of the corridor when the narrow strip of yellow light flared out from wall to wall. The figure was opening the door of the large room, and before Austin realized it, he had stepped through the arched opening to the other side of the wall into the living room.

# Chapter 4

Just inside the living room, Austin stood paralyzed. No move to make; no breath to take. But he knew he couldn't wait too long. He exerted himself to make his legs move again and began to walk slowly toward a single sliding glass door, the other entrance to the large room.

On this side of the wall was the living room/dining room and the kitchen. The latter one shared a wall with the large room.

Austin kept turning his head back and forth, not knowing where the danger would come from. He heard the footsteps coming from the large room moments earlier, and the floor under his feet fueled his fear that his steps could be heard too. Each time he took a step, he first placed his foot on the floor then applied his bodyweight ever so lightly, as if he were treading on eggshells. The parquet here turned out to be quiet enough, but Austin was even worried about the creaking of his arthritic knees. Holding his gun in front of him, he glanced into the large room through the opening by the sliding door and spotted Sam.

Sam was lying on the floor between his desk and the corner sofa. He was not moving. Reddish-black blood was pooling on his back and trickling down toward his armpit from a gaping hole near his scapula.

The unknown figure had murdered Sam.

Austin had been awfully scared when he had spotted the figure through the other door, but the sight of the dead, bleeding body put the fear of death into him. He had gotten knifed once in his teenage years and had also suffered a severe car crash, but he had never felt anything like this before. He instantly stepped back from the door and ducked behind the kitchen island.

His chest was throbbing; his body was in a cold sweat. Each second struck him like it could be his last. Austin had headed over here today aware of what he was about to risk, and he had managed to convince himself that his life wouldn't be included. He had figured that as long as he could hold his gun in front, he would not end up with a disadvantage. But this thought, built on fear and doubt, now crumbled. The kitchen had an L-shaped layout, and the island, or rather the "peninsula," was attached to the wall for space saving. Its closure provided cover for Austin, and he no longer had to look behind his back, at least.

He tried to compose himself and started to contemplate his predicament and the possible ways out. He recalled what he had seen and heard in the past few minutes, ever since the moment the corridor had lit up, searching for the answer to the most burning question—*did he see me?*

He tried to figure out whether he had managed to disappear behind the living room wall in time. The memory of that very second kept flashing in his mind, and he replayed it through to the last frame, again and again. He remembered the figure opening the door and the three holes in the figure's ski mask. But he couldn't recall what he had seen behind two of those holes. He had not caught whether the eyes behind the mask were looking at him, but he couldn't convince himself that they weren't. Nor could he figure out if he had given himself away by making noise afterwards.

Before Austin had ducked behind the kitchen island, he had glanced toward the arched opening, and the yellow light

13

seemed to have drawn back from the corridor. Perhaps the figure had closed the door behind himself. But he couldn't recall any sound of that either. And the most maddening part was not being able to decide whether it was because no such thing happened or because he just hadn't heard it.

Therefore, the unknown gunman could still be anywhere in the house. However, there was no concrete sign to either confirm or reject this. Austin did not hear any more steps from the corridor, and he didn't hear the sound of the main entry door closing. He figured he would have. He had been able to hear steps coming from the room at the end of the corridor when he had been standing right there with a hat covering his ears, so he should have heard the rest too, if there had been any. At least, this is what Austin kept repeating to himself.

Minutes passed one after the other. During his field checks, Austin thoroughly scanned the house, so he knew he wouldn't find another exit. He also studied the only window in the kitchen: a small, oblong awning window between the sink and the cabinets. Austin thought he might be able to push himself through it, but only if he had been on a diet for a few weeks, which he hadn't, and if there were no window frame, which there was. He tried to keep it together, even though his entire body was burning up and in a cold sweat.

He focused his thoughts on the large room and, especially, the narrow balcony just outside it. He tried to picture and estimate the distance to the slope below the balcony. Despite hours of watching the house and even more hours leaning over photos he had taken of the house, right now, it was quite difficult to determine exactly. Yet, the memories he managed to gather were sufficient enough for him to arrive at a conclusion—it was too high to jump off. The slope was way too steep, and it was blanketed with coarse rock.

Most likely, he would crash, which wouldn't contribute much to his escape. Getting out of the house wasn't enough though. He also would have to somehow get off the mountain with a gun barrel pointed at his back.

At this point, he thought about the large window in the living room. He could easily fit through it, even sideways, but according to his memory, he would still fall several feet if he jumped out. Because of the steepness of the slope, it would be about half of the way down from the balcony. It seemed to be a much better option but still a desperate one, because if he approached the window, he could get hit with a bullet out of nowhere at any time. Maybe he could charge toward it from the side, from between the table and the couch, and simply smash through the glass. A few film scenes stormed in his mind in which various heroes fell through all sorts of windows of their own free will, or not.

An awful realization hit Austin—this was not a movie. This was terribly real. Nevertheless, not one single window popped into his head that had posed any kind of obstacle to any hero ever. That being considered, he still pictured his own impaled body hooked on the glass shards that were pointing out of the frame like blades. Even if he ran to it with full speed or threw something at it, he wouldn't know beforehand if the glass was weak enough to shatter and open up a path for his flying leap. Of course, he did not forget about the gun in his hand. Putting a bullet through the window must be enough to make the glass comply. This idea just triggered more movie clips to run through his head, some of which had entire glass panels shattering to pieces from a single shot, while others showed each round creating only a tiny hole in the glass, depending on what the movie plot required.

But even if he chose to be deeply optimistic and were to bet on the scenario in which the window wouldn't be a problem, there was still the scree slope at the end of the falling, and while on the other side, the figure in black and his gun. Of course, there was a chance Austin could challenge the figure, as he was not particularly unarmed either. However, unlike in a movie, if he made a mistake here, there would be no second chance. No matter which one he chose—door, window or balcony—he was betting on his life, but unfortunately, none of the choices had good odds. The question was, of course, how good could the odds be when you are lying low on the kitchen floor with a murderer in the house? But Austin came to the conclusion that as long as he didn't force the figure to make a move, and the figure stayed on the other side of that wall, then the kitchen might be the safest of all.

As Austin was sitting on the floor, the police popped into his head as a lifesaving and also life-derailing option. The doubts that came along with this were lining up a mile behind the fact that he had nothing in hand to call anyone or anything. Therefore, it was the prospect of his own dead body that kept him terrified, rather than the question of what would happen if the police were to find him here with one. Because if the gunman had seen or heard him right after shooting someone, there was no way he would just walk away.

But what if there was? Even if the shooter had seen him, he was wearing a full-face mask, after all. Even if he left a witness behind, that person could never identify him. Then why not just leave the scene? This question raised a similar one—why didn't the murderer leave the house much earlier? Austin had been watching the only entrance to the house, and he hadn't seen anyone coming or going. Plus, he had not heard a gunshot when he had snuck in. So, what was the killer doing waiting in the large room with a dead body for so long? But Austin quickly stopped himself from this line of thinking, saying to himself: *It's not the time to investigate, who cares what he's doing?* Austin knew he just needed to survive. Either someone in the house was trying to silence him, or no one was here, and he was scared, huddling on the ground, and gripping his gun while there was a dead body in the next room—for no reason at all.

The cold kitchen floor offset the heat spreading through Austin's body. Without a watch and a phone, he couldn't tell exactly how long he'd been sitting there. But he ultimately decided to try something, an idea, an option that had been stirring at the back of his eyes for a while. He knew trying it would put a lot at risk.

# Chapter 5

"Hey!" Austin called out, his voice shaking.

No one responded, but Austin continued.

"Listen . . . if you're still there . . . I have no idea who you are, and I don't care . . . But I'm not with Sam. I came shortly after you. And I don't want any trouble, don't want anything. I snuck in here too, so I won't fuckin' go to the police, if that's what you're afraid of. And I didn't see your face, so I can't identify you anyway. I just wanna get out of here. Just as you do, I suppose."

Austin stopped here for a couple of seconds and listened. Only silence.

"You hear me? I think none of us wanted any of this. But it's not too late. You did what you came for—oh God . . ." Austin broke down, horrified and scared. "I just wanna go home . . . What do you think? We go our separate ways and forget all of this."

Not a single word came from behind the wall.

*You still here, God damn it??* Austin listened intently, holding his breath to hear the slightest, tiniest noise from the other side or anywhere else in the house. Long minutes passed, but he heard nothing. The real problem was that he couldn't know if this was good or bad for him. If he bet that the gunman was no longer there and took the risk of going outside, he could come to grief very easily. Even if the gunman had left the house, there was no guarantee he was actually gone. Maybe he was just trying to lure Austin outside and was waiting for him somewhere in the dark by one of the walls of the house or behind a bush. Maybe the shooter had been hiding outside long enough to know how easy it was to remain unseen. Inside, in his corner, Austin could be surprised from fewer directions than if he were outside. Running down the narrow mountain road or floundering amongst the trees, Austin could be awarded with a bullet from anywhere at any time.

Austin stopped trying to talk to the other side of the wall and paid no more attention to the passage of time. Instead, he silently pondered his situation, going through the possible solutions, while still listening, watching.

Slowly, he began to calm down. Of course, he was not even close to being totally calm, but at least his fear of dying dropped slightly due to the absence of any signs of an immediate threat. He was able to think more clearly, and as a result, he started focusing on the balcony as an option again. Assuming the assailant hadn't gone anywhere and was silent in order to force Austin to make a mistake, the balcony seemed logical. If the figure was in the house now, then he must be in the corridor because it was the only way of watching the one actual exit—the entrance. Maybe the murderer was at the doorway of one of the small rooms and had the door ajar as cover. But surely, he wasn't hiding deep inside any of the rooms. Especially not the one that was well lit and had exterior walls made mostly of glass. At least, that was the conclusion Austin made by putting himself in the killer's shoes.

On the other hand, if the murderer was waiting outside, he was still more likely to be watching the entrance than poised on the slope waiting for Austin to jump. Nope. With all the dangers of falling, using the balcony as an escape route seemed the least of the worst. It held the lowest risk of encountering a bullet on the way.

Austin leaned forward and carefully pressed himself close to the end of the kitchen island. He was thinking that if he could somehow sneak into the large room and see that no one was waiting for him except Sam's dead body, then he'd be in a slightly better position. The two doors of the large room were basically next to each other, so Austin could continue to watch only one direction. He could find plenty of cover in there and might be able to work out how to jump and land safely. He tried to glance into the room again, hoping he could get a proper look at the couch Sam was lying next to. If the cushions could be removed, then maybe he could just drop one onto the slope to land on. If he did it quick enough and the cushions softened his landing enough so that he didn't break his legs, then he had a much better chance of escape. Or even better, maybe he could jump with the cushion and land softly in a Jason Bourne style. This way, he would make a thudding noise only once, leaving even less time for the murderer to react, wherever he was.

After landing, Austin could start hightailing it to the bushes in the dark. And if the shooter appeared just a few seconds late and failed to gun Austin down on the slope before Austin disappeared into the dense trees, then he wouldn't stop, even to catch a breath, until his own doorstep. The murderer probably would not go after him, given that he would lose the advantages of his current location—silence and walls. In a chase outside, the element of surprise could switch the advantage anytime. And maybe this was the thing that the gunman was not so keen on risking.

What led Austin to this very conclusion was the fact that he hadn't been attacked yet. Which means the shooter must know that Austin had a gun, too. If he had seen Austin in the corridor, then he might also have seen what Austin had been holding in his hand. But if he hadn't seen Austin and had just heard him through the wall, then he had no way of knowing about his gun. And Austin had not given a hint in any form when he had talked to him about the situation. But there must be a reason why the shooter hadn't attacked him. So even if he didn't know for sure, he must be assuming that Austin had a gun.

Despite all the question marks and uncertainty, a plan started to take shape in Austin's head. If he chose the door, chances were that he'd exit the house as an open target. That's assuming he made it outside. All it would take is Austin being one second slower crossing the corridor, and he could be shot dead. But if he made it to the point that he was standing on his feet down there on the slope, then maybe he could rectify his current disadvantage. He had a gun, so he could even cover himself on the way to the woods.

Austin tried to calm his rapidly beating heart with this prospect, but it didn't show any intention of slowing down. There were still many more questions and pitfalls to each option, each one of them fueled by uncertainty. No matter how well Austin calculated, as long as he didn't know where the killer was, the killer could be anywhere. And with every move, from pacing to messing with the cushions, Austin might make enough noise to give himself away. Then he might share Sam's fate, and judging by the bloodstain, Sam hadn't even had time to turn around.

But Austin knew he had to overcome his fear that glued him to this kitchen floor. He had to try his luck with one of his options. And that would be the large room and the balcony. So he decided; he would wait no longer.

Austin's gun barrel inched out from behind the kitchen island first, then Austin himself peered out. He could not see any incongruous shadows or anything else worthy of suspicion. He leaned forward a couple more inches to see inside the large room. Every drop of Austin's blood froze in his veins.

Sam's body had disappeared.

# Chapter 6

Sam had always had a thing for heights. But only when it was paired with a sense of security. He'd never felt the need to try skydiving or bungee jumping, and he didn't even particularly enjoy airplane travel. He enjoyed seeing the world from high places that weren't moving. So much so that perhaps this was the sole activity that turned him no profit of any kind but kept him occupied for long hours. That says quite a lot about a person with the tendency to text or do business even during movies and sporting events.

He even ignored the advice of his lead architect when he told Sam to look for a spot on a lower slope to build his new home, due to the "far from ideal" features of his preferred location. Sam hadn't been discouraged by the thought of extending the duration of the construction nor the ballooning cost. He didn't make the lead architect's life easy, for sure. But Sam wasn't the kind of guy who couldn't be reasoned with, either, so they eventually managed to find common ground. The house was designed so that it would rest on the tallest pillars and float the furthest above the slope, while staying strictly within reasonable architectural boundaries and safety limits. He even once noted it to the architect, "They are called 'floating houses' for a reason, so let them float." The floor space ended up around 2200 square feet, and the external pillars reached almost 30 feet, which completely satisfied Sam.

Despite the beautiful view of the valley and the city lying in the center, Sam didn't want to build a glass box. Although, the large room on the front might suggest otherwise. He preferred more closed, private interior spaces but since the nearest prying eyes were miles away, he allowed his wife to talk him into using more glass for the large room, at least. Sam would have been perfectly fine with concrete walls all around. To enjoy the view, he would simply sit out on the balcony with a bottle and a glass or a cup, depending on the hour. That is why Sam's house had more concrete than glass, especially in comparison to other houses built on slope. The kitchen, for instance, was honored with only a small, oblong window between the sink and the wall cabinets. Even less lucky for the small bedroom, that had no window at all, thanks to the exterior stairway between the rooftop and the main entrance. It wouldn't have made any sense to punch a hole in the bedroom wall since all you'd see was the stairs and the concrete wall that hid the stairs from the outside world. Good question, though, how much sense could be found in the concept of a windowless bedroom in a hillside house. And the answer to that could be found in none other than Sam. After all, whoever in his position got a certain use from their weekend house, which he did, could no doubt benefit from a windowless bedroom.

The large room sat right above the slope and was the full width of the house. There were two doors to this room. They were situated right next to each other, across from the floor-to-ceiling windows, in the center of the wall that divided the house in half. One door came from the kitchen, the other from the corridor. In the center of the windows, the most massive pillar of the house continued up through the floor to the ceiling, jutting out from the wall and creating two areas of the room. Facing the windows, the right was Sam's bedroom and gym with a double bed, and an exercise bike. The left half was a kind of study, with a sectional sofa, display cabinet, and an elegant coffee table. The famous workstation was between the sofa and the pillar and was separated from the balcony by a floor-to-ceiling concrete wall. And since the exercise bike was right on the other side of the pillar, just in front of the window, Sam sometimes joked that he actually worked on both sides, so the workroom title to this large room totally fit.

Sam's minimalistic taste could be seen in everything he owned, from his house to his car to his desk. Everything was tasteful, elegant, and free of any flashiness and unusual shapes. If it wasn't for his wife, Lindsey, the walls wouldn't be decorated with as many landscapes and photos of cities and buildings. No wonder only one picture qualified to be in the large room, a sunset tinting a major city in a beautiful golden-yellow light. As Sam saw it, Lindsey preferred the city, and Sam preferred the nature, so the combination of these two in one picture was more than enough in the large room. And, as could be seen by looking at the walls, Lindsey accepted it.

\*\*\*

Light had not penetrated the darkness yet, but noises had already begun to disrupt the silence. These were very quiet noises and barely detectable—breathing and the friction between floor and clothing. Sam regained his consciousness, but it took him a few seconds to open his eyes. At first, he didn't know where he was or what had happened. Only the blurred backside of the beige sofa looked familiar. Then, the events leading up to when he had hit the ground began to dawn on him as his right palm and forearm started to ache. He feared turning his head over, but he quickly realized that the tiny, twinging pains were being caused by splinters of the glass that had slipped out of his fingers when he had fallen on the ground. The small shards had dug themselves into his palm and the part of his forearms that had been left uncovered by his rolled-up sleeves. His left hand was still in his pants pocket. The pants were too tightly tailored to release Sam's hand when he had needed it to buffer the impact of his fall. But he knew that the prickly glass pieces were the least of his problem. He had, in fact, gotten shot!

He carefully rolled his head around, examining the area around him, but he could not find a pool of blood. That led him to the conclusion that the bullet hadn't traveled all the way through his body. *It's sitting inside my back*, he thought. He pulled his left hand out of his pocket in order to gain some leverage to get up from the floor, but a stabbing pain announced itself in his back. *Oh my God*, he thought, *my spine*. He quickly checked himself below the belt. Great relief took over as he felt both of his legs moving from hip to toe. Then, as Sam was turning his face back toward his right shoulder, he spotted a moving shadow in the kitchen, the source of which must have been hiding from his eyes behind the kitchen island. His assailant was still here!

This caused his heart to beat more intensely, and he felt it even stronger because his chest was pressed against the floor under his massive torso. All he needed to do was to reprise his role of the deceased, and he'd be fine. But why was the shooter still here? Looking for something? If so, who knows when he would leave. And whatever the answer was, he might not be able to afford the time in his situation, that is, lying on the floor with a hole in his back. Only his back, if he was lucky.

Then he thought of the top drawer of his desk. It was only a long reach away. He knew it could take only one bad moment, one in which he drew the gunman's attention to the fact that he was not dead, and everything would cease to matter. Then, he would actually be dead. But he chose to risk it.

He slid to the side a bit, careful enough to not make any noise with the glass splinters on the floor. He ignored the pain completely. While keeping an eye on the kitchen, he carefully reached over to the drawer, opened it, and lifted out his gun, a Glock 19. It was loaded, as always. Not the most textbook way of storing a firearm but something to be deeply grateful for now. As soon as he felt the gun in his hand, he pushed in the drawer and lay back in the dead position.

Then, he contemplated what to do. His chances had significantly improved, but his situation was still critical. He figured it would be unwise to conduct a shootout until he fully understood how much control he had over his body. On top of that, his head was lying in a different position, and it could easily give him away. Let alone his right palm, which was now resting on the grip of his handgun. His desk provided partial cover, but that wasn't life insurance. However, if he were to lie in his original position, facing the sofa, eyes closed or not, he would put himself back at a grave disadvantage. There was no other way—he must give up his current position and get going.

He watched the kitchen for a few seconds, then he braced himself and cautiously lifted his torso up from the floor and kneeled. Slowly, though trying to hurry, he crawled behind the sofa and froze, waiting to see if he could hear any noise that indicated someone had noticed his "resurrection". He was focused so intently on the noises that he had forgotten to check his upper body for exit wounds. And he had forgotten to unlock his gun. However, he heard nothing—no human voices, no steps, nothing.

On his knees and using his left arm as a crutch, Sam gingerly inched himself all the way along the back of the L-shaped sofa until he reached its other end. As much of a massive piece of furniture it was, Sam didn't fool himself into believing it could stop bullets. Still, it was a cover, and from there, he had a good view of the two doors. If the shooter were to use either door to enter the room, or even just put an arm inside, Sam could open fire.

Many parts of his body were aching like hell, but Sam tried as hard as he could to prevent his pain from squeezing any kind of noise out of him. Even so, he knew it was only a matter of time before his assailant discovered that his body was missing, although Sam might have just picked the best possible spot for that scenario. If the stranger were to enter the room and look at the spot where he'd left Sam, he'd likely cast his next glance toward the balcony, thinking the "dead" could have only fled that way. At that moment, Sam could easily surprise the gunman from this corner. At least, he used this thought to comfort himself.

But now, having secured a strong defensive position, he felt the time had come to take care of his bullet wound. While he kept his guard up by constantly glancing at the doors, Sam checked his upper body by sight and feel. No wound or any sign of one on the front of his body. The front of his shirt was intact, and there were no bloodstains on it. It seemed he had been right about the bullet still being inside his body. The hole it punched, however, must be taken care of.

Due to his current lack of access to medical care, Sam had to improvise something. He slowly removed his belt and buckled it up to his torso, tying it tightly all around his left armpit and up to the right side of his neck. He quietly took off one of his shoes and removed his sock. Not the most hygienic gauze material, but that's the best he could do. He winced as he tucked his sock between his belt and the wound and tightened the belt by one more hole. Perhaps the most low- cost tourniquet ever. He slipped back into his shoe, gently leaned against the cabinet, and waited. Every single nerve in his system focused on the two doors.

# Chapter 7

As he crouched behind the kitchen island, his body shaking, Austin felt like his head was about to split apart even though only two questions pressed it from the inside: *Where is Sam?* And: *Where the hell is the guy who shot him?* He didn't have answers to these, however a third question had arisen: How come he hadn't heard anything? Maybe if his head wasn't covered from the top of his head to his shoulders, he would've caught the sound of Sam rising from the dead.

*But it doesn't matter now,* Austin thought. *Sam got up. He's alive! Or maybe the guy dragged Sam's body away? But what sense would that have made? He wanted to sweep the crime scene? Then why start with the dead body, and not the living witness? It doesn't add up. No. Sam is alive. This is the more probable explanation. And if it is true, that might be good news since then there was no murder.*

He tried his best to prevent himself from losing the rest of his sanity. *Probably Sam is still in the room, hiding behind something,* he thought. *Or slipped out to the balcony? Or the corridor, using the other door and went straight outside from there and—?*

"How much for you to let me go?"

The excruciating maelstrom of doubts and questions in Austin's head went dead silent. The heaving voice had come from the large room. Some of Austin's questions had just met answers, at least. But all of a sudden, he was the shady figure hiding in silence. A role he wasn't in the mood to take on at all.

*** 

Sam had no way of knowing whether his attacker had discovered that he was no longer where he had fallen. And although Sam was aware that he essentially told the attacker which part of the room he was in, he felt the situation required him to initiate. Too much time had passed; the silence was too dead, and sadly, his time was certainly passing faster than the other's. Or fair to say, the other one's was just passing, while his was running out.

Without knowing the other one's whereabouts, Sam didn't dare to step outside the large room. He was waiting for an answer, although he knew there wasn't much of a chance for any kind of agreement. Not anymore. Unless he could convince the figure that he would be able to talk the hospital doctors into not being too interested in the bullet they were about to remove from his body. It didn't seem like a real possibility to Sam. But he couldn't know how the other one was thinking.

"Hey! You hear me? How much you want?" Sam tried again. "There's a safe in this room. Whatever's inside, all yours . . . One million. At least."

The grip of Austin's Ruger was about to crack under his fingers. He had not shot Sam, but he had come for what was in the safe. What should he say now? Or should he even say anything? For the second time tonight Austin had to face this very dilemma. Hiding from a threat tends to require staying silent, unless there is a chance to negotiate.

"Come on, I know, you're there. And you bet, we can work this out. Make everyone happy."

Sam was convinced that whoever had shot him had not come for what was in the safe, improbable at least, so he had to talk him into allowing the money to override his original plan. Maybe the shooter was working for someone who might not have paid as much as he just offered.

"Wasn't me who shot you," Sam suddenly heard from near the kitchen.

Sam was prepared for many kinds of responses, including silence, but this one was not one of them. He had to think for a moment about what to do with this information, then he continued.

"Listen, pal, I don't know what you want, but I'm telling you, we can—"

"It wasn't me who shot you!" Austin repeated with slightly more volume. He figured he had to risk audible communication again. His first attempt with the shooter didn't work but didn't get Austin killed either. Now he had to try with Sam. "It was someone else. And he's still in the house."

Austin wasn't fully certain the shooter was still in the house, but it didn't matter because either way, he had to act like it was true.

Sam was so jolted by the voice's words that he forgot about the pain stabbing his back, if only for a few refreshing seconds.

"What?!" Sam said.

"I saw him in your room. The door was open. He wore a mask. And he's still here. Somewhere."

*He's really trying to make me believe this?* "Why would he still be here? Why didn't leave straight away?"

"Because I think he saw me on the way out. And, I guess, he didn't wanna leave a witness behind."

"You said he wore a mask. Then why does it matter?"

"I don't know, ask him!"

Austin felt handicapped. He couldn't prove it from the kitchen, and he wasn't even sure if the shooter was still here. However, his last sentence gave him an idea.

"Didn't you hear me talking to someone?" Austin asked.

"Nope. No one was talking to nobody."

*Shit! He must've woken up afterwards.* "How long you been conscious?"

"A while, don't know." Sam had been in the dark about how much time had passed ever since he had stopped that bullet with his back.

"You must still have been unconscious when—"

"And what did you two talk about? If I may ask."

"He never answered," Austin said, elegantly skipping his own part. "But I know he's here."

"Ahhh . . ."

Sam sounded skeptical, which he was. At least now he could tell where the guy was by the sound of his voice, so he thought he could move around. He could go to the next room or even get out of the house through the corridor.

But he didn't. He tried to push himself, though, to go for it, to go to the next room, at least. But the words of the stranger, weirdly, kept him where he was. Even if there was a minor chance to it, what if he wasn't lying? What if someone was really waiting for him on the other side of the wall?

After he thought for a moment, Sam decided to play along with the game, or whatever this was. As long as he could keep the guy talking to him, he would know roughly where he was. Even if he wasn't going anywhere, keeping this advantage would certainly do him some good, along with the fact that he could guard both doors simultaneously.

"Alright," Sam said. "So you're trying to tell me that two people who don't know each other and never talked to each other picked the same day, almost the same minute, to break into my house and kill me?"

"I don't wanna kill you!!" Austin yelled.

"Yeah, whatever. The point is you came here at the same time. That's what you're saying."

"I know how it must sound, but I swear it's the truth."

"Okay, fine. Lucky you didn't crash into each other coming through the door."

Austin realized if he wasn't going to sketch a believable idea of how such coincidence could have happened, he might as-well quit swearing. If he were Sam, he wouldn't believe it, either. All the more so because he did not understand it himself.

"Maybe he was watching you," Austin said. "Maybe he was waiting for you to come home, somewhere outside, I don't know."

"And you?"

Austin quickly pondered the consequences of giving and not giving an answer.

"I just . . . followed you."

"From where?"

"Don't worry about that right now."

"Don't you fuckin' tell me what to worry about!"

"I just—"

"Okay, fine, you wouldn't tell me anyway, leave it, I'll ask something else. If your guy is really here, then what is he waiting for? Huh? He can obviously hear that I'm alive. So why isn't he coming to finish the job?"

"I . . . I really don't know." Austin was utterly clueless.

"There it is. That would be such a help though . . . But let's say you're telling the truth and really don't wanna kill me. Then why don't you come in here? You're obviously here as a friend, and what's more, a savior tonight, right? Isn't that so?"

"I'm not here to chum up, either. But you have my word, I don't wanna kill you."

"Then what . . ." Sam squirmed from his wound. "What do you want from me?"

"I . . . I just wanted money. Just money."

"Ah. Okay . . . fine. Then just put your gun down and come in. The safe is in this room. I tell you the combination, you take the money, and off you go."

"Deal. If you put down your gun, too."

"I don't have a gun."

"Why should I believe that? Because you'll swear? Just like I did?"

Sam didn't answer.

"There it is," Austin said.

"Okay then, just stay there and continue twiddling."

Not counting the risky escape, Austin had no better plan for the next few minutes, anyway. He was chewing over whether the other guy could've heard Sam saying that he's got no gun, and surely, he did, so then would he go for another try? It might be worth some waiting. Although, there was a good chance that he wouldn't believe him, or better yet, he knows about Sam's gun.

Because Austin was well aware of the gun Sam kept in this house. But he didn't want to let on. He didn't know which room Sam kept it in, anyway. He could only assume that the gun was in the same room where Sam was now, and he could especially assume that Sam had managed to get it and was holding it right now.

"Hey, you! Wherever you are," Sam shouted suddenly and quite loudly. "I'm talkin' to you, dear other stranger who broke into my home today. The thing is, I can't really do business with this one, here," he said, referring to Austin. "But what about you? Whatever it is you're after, I can assure you, there's enough money in the safe for you to reconsider things. You can leave as a rich man. Way richer than when you got here. And you won't be wanted for murder. Or at least you'll be wanted for one less murder. What do you say?"

Sam had to be satisfied with dead silence as an answer, just as Austin had earlier.

"I already prefer your pal more than you. He doesn't talk that much," Sam mocked.

"Listen, if I really want to kill you, and I missed at first, then tell me, what is it I'm waiting for? Why don't I just casually walk over and put a bullet in your head?"

"Maybe because you refuse to believe that I don't have a gun on me and you don't wanna take your chances in a gunfight. Because you expected an unarmed man who you could shoot in the back and then casually walk away. And you might've missed, but you know you hit me. So . . . maybe you're just biding your time and waiting for me to bleed or pass out."

*It might not be such a bad idea. If I went silent,* Sam thought, *he surely would come in here to check.*

Austin was about to be driven crazy. Regarding the gun, Sam hit the nail in the head, but everything else he said about the real attacker was probably utterly true. And for all Austin knew, he could be smiling from ear to ear under his mask on the other side. If he was even still there.

"You know what? I don't believe it," Austin replied, quite edgy.

"Then don't."

36

"Unarmed, in a situation like this, sure, you wouldn't have such a big mouth."

"You think so?"

"You'd have jumped the fuck off the balcony a while ago, not caring about how far you fell."

"If you say so."

"I say so! And also, I don't think you'd have given up posing as a dead in the first place. Because what for? To give away you're still alive, for nothing? Nah, you'd have stayed on your belly and stayed quiet. At least, as long as you could hear someone in the house. But a gun and a good cover, that's something might be worth risking for . . . Or not?"

"Impressive logic."

"But now, you tell me something. If I shot you, why didn't I just take off straight away? Before you woke up."

"Maybe you were looking for something."

"What exactly?"

"You tell me."

"Already told you, asshole. I came for your money!"

"I know you told me. Or maybe you just said that because it's obvious to say, but you were actually looking for something else."

"Oh yeah, and I'd rather shoot you and rummage through the whole house, instead of just gun-forcing you to give it over, right?"

Now Sam fell into contemplation. "Maybe you thought you knew where to look for it, so no need to risk it."

Austin stayed silent.

"But you know what?" Sam asked. "Forget it. We should first find out how many of us are here. If you stick to your story."

"I told you—"

"That you're not the one who shot me! Even if that's true, you can't prove that your man is still here. At least, you failed so far. I even got the feeling that you're not quite sure yourself. So how about you, just going around in the house and find out?"

"I would, believe me."

"Then what are you waiting for? You got a gun, no?"

"Yep. But I'm scared to risk it."

"Ah, you're scared. I see. And I'm supposed to believe that's the only reason you're sitting so tight over there with a gun in your hand?"

*And what if it turns out, there's nobody here?* Austin thought. *Then how can I convince him it wasn't me? But then, I just get the hell out of here. Hoping I won't get hit by the other one and somehow get far enough from here before the police are swarming the whole mountain.*

"Silence is not helping now, buddy," Sam said, interrupting Austin's thoughts. "You didn't expect resistance and now you're shitting your pants. Actually, I can be generous and believe all that. But won't change a thing. Either you flash a third person to me, or we won't become friends, I'm afraid."

And then an idea popped into Austin's head that he hadn't thought of until this moment and he didn't want to believe.

"You got a phone on you?" he asked.

"Nope." *Not that I'd tell you.*

"It's somewhere in the house then?"

"Left it in the car—the fuckin' car!" Sam was frustrated to say the least. "But that's a good one to bring up. Do me a favor and go get it for me. I actually have an important call to make."

Austin hoped that Sam's cynical humor was an indication that their cause was not completely hopeless. But some heavy doubts instantly came to this picture.

"How can I know that . . ." Austin left the sentence unfinished, realizing that it was pointless to finish.

"That I'm not playing you? Well, looks like this is the question of the day. Maybe I already called the cops, discretely, and they'll be here any minute. So maybe you'd better fuck off as fast as you can."

"You say so?"

"Yep. Couldn't identify you anyway. And same goes for everyone, no matter how many you are!"

Sam finished the sentence shouting. He knew how risky this little bluff was since it could very well urge the shooter to move and try to kill him quickly before making his escape. Sam was still sitting behind the sofa, steadily holding up his gun, his eyes glued to the doors.

Austin's stomach started to feel queasy. *What if the police really are on their way?* Easier to get freed from prison than a cemetery, after all. He wondered what the other one was making of Sam's last sentences, if he were still in the house. If the shooter didn't make a move, then maybe he shouldn't either for now. Or maybe the shooter won't do anything because he knows something or doesn't believe Sam. Or he's simply not here at all. The latter option was the one that made Austin feel like he was ready to lose it. But unfortunately, he couldn't afford to cut it off from any of his lines of thought. Nothing was for certain—Sam's phone, his gun, the other one's whereabouts . . . Under these circumstances, there was no possible solution he could go with.

After thinking about it, Austin decided to believe that Sam hadn't had the chance to call for help yet. It seemed more likely so he went with that to start.

"Okay, let's say you really don't have your phone on you and didn't call the police."

"Let's say,' Sam repeated sharply.

"If I let you call them, would you believe me?"

"Of course," Sam answered, slightly surprised. "Why? You have your phone?"

"Nope."

"Thought not."

"Fine. I know you don't believe it."

"No, I do believe that. I wouldn't bring one on a mission like this, either. What I don't believe is that you'd simply just pass it to me."

Austin didn't rush answering. "Yeah . . . Unlikely indeed," he finally said.

"Hm . . ." Sam hummed. "And if I give you my word that you'll get it back after and you're free to go?"

"And I'm supposed to believe that, right?"

"You're supposed to believe that I want nothing else but all the armed dicks to get the hell out of my house and have a doctor here to save my fuckin' life!" Sam was raging a bit and letting out some steam. "So, yeah, I'd give it back."

Austin did not say a word. Sam continued talking in a bit calmer tone.

"But actually, you could call them on my behalf . . . And you don't even have to be here. You can call on your way down. There's reception, so . . .'

"Even if I believed you and had enough time to disappear, I'm still no cop, okay?"

"What?"

"What's the procedure—just standing there, scratching heads or maybe they identify the cell and in ten minutes they get to the person who owns it. Me. Even if I destroy it—but

40

who cares?? I told you I got no phone. And why I'm still sitting on my ass in your kitchen—"

"Okay, okay, easy, I get it, fine," Sam soothed Austin. "Forget it."

Austin calmed down as best he could and kept thinking. Or rather he tried to use his head instead of abusing it by smashing it into the wall. Because he had just realized that if the sight of Sam's body on the floor hadn't terrified him then he would've sought cover in the large room, instead of the kitchen, and he probably wouldn't have missed Sam waking up. That way, in Sam's first minutes awake, he could have cleared himself, and they could have teamed up. But since all his efforts went to stopping himself from falling apart— he tried to divert his thoughts far away from it.

Possible solutions kept swirling in this head. Searching the rest of the house was off the table, especially after discussing it out loud with Sam. If the shooter was still there, he would anticipate this. But if Austin managed to slip out quickly, made it up to the roof and the car, took the same way back in but with the phone in his hand for Sam, he would certainly earn Sam's trust. Although, there were several problems with that. First, this slipping out didn't seem any less dangerous now than when it had first occurred to him.

"So . . . it's gotta be my phone, then." Sam pitched the idea once again.

"Still thinking."

"Uh, no rush. Take your time."

Then, Sam realized he could call for help on his laptop. Message his wife, a friend, or videocall them, tell them he's in trouble, call the police.

"Listen. There might be another way. I got my laptop on the desk. I can use that to get help. So let's make a deal—you let me go get it, then we gonna be friends. Plus, you'll get the money."

"Do it!" Austin replied at once.

Sam tried to figure out why the other one nodded on this idea without thinking. He wants to lure him out to the middle of the room to make an easier target, or he really means it. Sam felt he had to try either way. Sam spent a few moments trying to remove the glass splinters still stuck in his right palm. It wasn't totally necessary; he could have used the gun with his left hand. But the bleeding, aching right hand was still the preferred one.

Sam took a deep breath and slowly started to move to try to make it all the way back behind the sofa. Austin was patiently sitting behind the island listening. He had to hand it to Sam; he was able to move that tall, bear-like, injured body quite noiselessly along the floor. It didn't take Sam long to reach the other end of the sofa. He carefully positioned himself so he could point his face toward the kitchen while keeping one eye on the door to the corridor. He saw nobody. He figured if the other one, or ones, went for a try now, the sofa would hardly stop a fired bullet, so the cover was sort of an illusion. Hence, his eyes were constantly on the doors.

In a half-squat behind the sofa, Sam stretched forward over the sofa until his left hand could grab the computer screen. Ignoring the sharp pain, he pulled the machine to himself, the plug letting go without a fight. Sam didn't care about the charger. He saw no point in risking the crawl to the socket on the other side of the desk. There wasn't one to plug into around his corner anyway, and by his estimation, the laptop would last longer without a power supply than he would without medical treatment. With the laptop under his armpit, the gun in his hand, and one eye constantly on the doors, he knee-slid to the other end of the sofa. The moment he got there, still not caring about the pain, he slid his fingers on the touchpad, lighting up the screen. Sam instantly glanced at the bottom right corner—no internet connection.

*Damn it, not now!* He tried to reconnect multiple times, unsuccessfully. Trouble with the signal wouldn't be much of a surprise, but it wasn't Sam's first thought.

"Nice trick, asshole!"

"What?"

"No internet."

"How?"

"Quite a mystery, huh?"

Austin instantly realized he was the one to blame. But instead of engaging in passionate self-defense, he began to think.

"Where is the router?"

"You don't know?"

"No, fuck's sake, answer me!"

"In the corridor."

Once again, Austin recalled the moments he had spent there. He couldn't remember all the fine details clearly, but there might have been, indeed, a small, black box, with lights on it, down on the left, in between the two doors. Austin couldn't tell for certain. But if the router was there, as Sam said, all the shooter would've had to do was bend down and switch it off after he had heard the two of them talking about the internet. *So he's gotta be here*, Austin thought.

"What's on the screen?" Austin asked Sam. "Just struggling around or no signal at all?"

"No signal."

"You sure?"

"I'm sure! It was good all evening, but now, suddenly ciao. How's that?"

Austin didn't say anything. He knew Sam blamed him. But he saw it as proof of there being three in here.

"I told you, there's someone else in here."

"And you think I'm now all convinced, right?"

"Why the hell would I mess with your stupid internet? And mostly, when?"

"Anytime when you had a half-minute window when we weren't chatting. And there was plenty of them."

*The other one certainly could have*, Austin thought. *He could've done it anytime, still left the house straight after, and was waiting outside.*

Sam did blame Austin for the dead internet connection. But somehow, the thought of the second "guest" refused to go away. Maybe the kitchen guy had never moved an inch. The other one could've easily switched off the router in the corridor. More so, it occurred to Sam that they might be working together. Either way, if there really was a third person here, then keeping the guy talking in the kitchen or anywhere else, wouldn't be much help. When the kitchen guy goes to get his phone, the other one could surprise him from any spot.

Austin concealed his growing temper and spoke again more calmly.

"Alright," he said, "go and switch it on."

"So you can rush in and install a bullet in my laptop? Or in me from any direction?"

"Fuck your laptop and fuck you!" Austin burst out. "If I wanted to, I could've gunned the shit out of your fucking laptop a long time ago. I had the perfect view for that from right fucking here. But if you're so worried, just put it under your armpit and bring it with you! Okay?"

Sam didn't reply.

"Just go, keep your eyes open, switch the net back on, and call 911 from there. I can't shoot through the wall anyway." *At least, I hope it wouldn't let the bullets through*, Austin thought since that wall was an important piece of protection for him, too. "And once you're there, you might as well get to your ride and drive away. Enough of this bullshit! You don't believe me, fine, I get it. Just move your ass and get out of here! If you want, I can sing for you, so you know all along where I am."

"Well, no doubt, I fancy the inside of a car the most right now," Sam said. "Ambulance would be the best but mine would do," Sam mocked, veiling his real thoughts. "But I'd rather be sitting even in the adjacent room," Sam muttered inaudibly. He hadn't become a believer of what Austin had been saying; he was simply becoming more convinced that Austin wasn't lying. But what exactly he was thinking, he didn't intend to share, at least for now, mostly because he didn't really know himself.

Sam suddenly realized that he was already fantasizing about what he would do if he got outside. To start running down would be lunacy. He'd be injured in the middle of nowhere. Who knows how long it would take to reach the first house that had somebody inside. No, if he made it outside on foot, he would try the car. Either way, he could be shot at any moment. He could be taking one look at the car keys or turning his face to the wrong direction. Dangerous. But so was it, of course, in here between the sofa and the cabinet. He knew his priority must be what to do while he was in the house, not out there.

Although, if the internet wouldn't come back, and it sure was looking that way, or if he were to fail to find another solution, then soon he was gonna have to take the risk and leave somehow. Otherwise, it was just a matter of time before he would bleed out.

# Chapter 8

Sam's eyes abandoned his watch of the two doors for a moment when he got distracted by the picture hanging above the workstation. What if it's not a sunset? he wondered. What if that's a sunrise? How can anyone tell the difference anyway? Whatever it was, it might be the last he would ever see in his life.

He came back down to the ground of reality, knowing he had to monitor how he was feeling, whether his condition was worsening, and how fast. He had been sweating more and more intensely as his system fought the blood loss, and now, dizziness had checked in.

While Sam was focusing on his symptoms, he was suddenly hit by the realization that there had been another several minutes of silence. This reminded him of the idea of playing dead, or passed out, didn't matter. Falling into complete silence would probably make the other guy want to check why.

But Sam shortly came to the conclusion that it wouldn't help much. *Unlikely the guy would just waltz into the room*, he thought, *even if I was lying on the floor.* But if the guy sticks just a half of his head in, with one eye showing, as he would, that wouldn't mean such a promising target. So Sam ditched the idea. For now.

The city occupied his thoughts for the next few silent minutes. Then he pictured himself somewhere in the valley. If he were similarly entrapped way down there, how much easier it would be to get help.

Sam stopped brooding and switched back to reality again. While he was staring at pictures and daydreaming, the clock was ticking and not to his benefit.

"Still here?" he asked Austin.

No answer.

"Hey! Are you still here?"

"Yeah, I'm here. Sorry."

Sam felt a quantum of relief when he heard that voice coming from the very same direction as before. Not that he welcomed the idea of having a gunman in his house, especially one who didn't seem very interested in leaving. Tonight, silence was carrying way more danger than any other time. The silence up here that Sam loved so much had turned against him. Silence tends not to be welcome in company, but this one was lethal, not awkward. That is why Sam couldn't afford to allow it to stretch on for too long.

"So, it means, you're still not in the mood for a walk to my car, right?"

"Right. You?"

"No. But fine. There's another way for you to convince me."

"What?"

"Pass me your gun."

Austin was amazed. From the other side, the idea made total sense.

"I can't. If that guy is still here, then I'm done. How am I supposed to protect myself?"

"If that guy is still here."

"Stop repeating what I'm saying. Anyway, I know you still don't believe me."

"If you give me your gun, I'll believe you."

"I just told you, I can't. I—"

"Wait!" Sam interrupted. "Then just swap guns."

"What's the point of that?"

"To see if yours was fired. If I don't smell gunpowder, then I can believe it wasn't you. And together we'll figure out what's next. Okay?"

*It isn't such a bad idea,* Austin thought. "And who's gonna throw first?"

"Well, I was thinking . . . you."

"Yeah, of course."

"I'm the one with a bullet in his back, so let me be the more cautious one."

"Sorry. I can't. I can't trust you."

"I'm telling you, if you just throw it over, and I figure out it wasn't fired, then I will believe it wasn't you. Or is it . . . that I would find otherwise?"

"No. You wouldn't."

"So, which is it?"

"If I were you, I wouldn't . . . I wouldn't dare take it for granted that there's only one gun."

"Huh," Sam said, dismayed for a moment. Lying or not about the other intruder, he found this surprisingly honest.

"But that's just me," Austin said. "But what if it's also you. Then it can cost me my life."

"Well, whether you're lying or not, tonight could easily cost you your life either way."

Austin did not react.

"So? You're not gonna pass me your piece?" Sam said.

"Sorry. I can't. But not because I wanna shoot you with it."

"Alright. Suit yourself." Sam actually understood. A few seconds of silence followed. "But in that case, would you do me another thing?"

"What?"

"You mind rolling over that bottle of gin from the counter? That won't cost you your life. But it can easily cost me mine if I don't have a sip.'

"Uh . . . sure," Austin answered reluctantly. He considered this request the same kind as the "pass over your gun" one, unexpected but reasonable. Still, he gave himself the courtesy of thinking it over for a minute. *Could be just a trick to make me stick my head out of my cover.* But even if it wasn't, Austin still had to stick his head out to pass the gin to Sam. He wasn't quite enthusiastic about that. At least the bottle was sitting on the kitchen side of the counter, really close to the edge, so Austin could reach it easily. A 0.7l Tanqueray in its dark-green bottle, the trademark dark-red Tanqueray wax-seal logo under the neck. The level of beverage was wavering around halfway between the cap and the bottom. Austin hesitated but then made up his mind.

"May I have a sip, too?"

"Of course, help yourself."

"Thanks."

Austin unscrewed the cap, took a deep sniff of the bottle, and quickly flushed a couple of large, burning gulps down his throat. Under normal circumstances, he'd never drink gin neat from the bottle. And thanks to the current, highly abnormal circumstances, he was even less capable of enjoying it. Still, this was the best thing that had happened to him that day by far, counting from the moment he left his bed at dawn until now. As far as Austin was concerned, getting out of bed was the only thing separating today from yesterday, as his eyes had been open all night.

He screwed the cap back and quietly squat-slinked to the end of the island, gun in the right hand, bottle in the left. Moving in a squatting position made him a bit wobbly, so he softly placed his right knee on the floor. At the same time, his eyes were continuously scanning the area between the large room's sliding door and the other side of the kitchen island. Resting on one knee, Austin leaned forward ever so slowly and poked his head out for one brief second. The dark living room did a great job of showing itself to be safe and peaceful. Even so, Austin's heart started pumping heavily just to remind him that he better get this whole operation over with as soon as possible.

He inched to the right to get a better angle toward the sliding-glass doorway and the part of the room where he expected to see Sam's hideout. He was still hidden from the living room by the island, but since he was closer to the trash can by the wall now, he was already getting a view of the other end of the sofa in the large room. Austin assumed Sam must be there because that's where Sam's voice had come from. He quickly switched the gun and the bottle in his hands, grabbed the bottle by the bottom, and released it to its voyage across the floor. There was no obstacle in the doorway since the sliding door was running on an upper rail, so the bottle slid smoothly into the room, bounced off a leg of the coffee table, and disappeared from Austin's sight.

Sam painstakingly lifted himself to a squatting position. His pain was getting worse, but fortunately, it took just a few steps to reach out, grab the bottle, and move back to his spot.

"Lucky for me, you aim better with a bottle than with a gun."

The best Austin could do was a semi-smile, but that wasn't the joke's fault.

"But thanks. My blessing," Sam added.

"And to you. Though would be better with tonic."

"Tell me about it. I forgot to buy it."

Like it was the nectar of the gods, Sam poured the gin down his throat, feeling it go all the way to his shrunken, empty stomach. Sam also realized that there might be another possible blessing effect of the booze. He held the bottle up behind his shoulder, blindly tried to aim, then poured a few shots worth of gin down his back, hoping it would run right into the wound under the sock. If the stuff he let stream down his throat shortened his life, he figured the stuff rolling down his back might extend it.

"You okay there?" Austin asked when he heard Sam's painful moans.

"Yeah, fine. It's just really strong without tonic."

It took some time for Austin to get the joke. Even when he did, his smile was still little more than a semi, but it contained a bit more honesty. What Sam had said made a bit of hope start to grow in Austin. As long as Sam was throwing out bits like this, there could be a chance for some sort of agreement.

Silence took charge again for a little while, but Sam couldn't endure it for long.

"What do I call you?" Sam asked. "I mean, you're obviously not gonna tell me your real name, so pick one."

"Buddy will do."

"Hmm, okay," Sam agreed, then gulped another one from the bottle, but didn't indulge his wound. "So, Buddy, why me?"

"What?"

"Why is it me you're trying to rip off? Did we cross each other before?"

"You understand, I don't wanna blab about myself, right? In case you make it outta here alive."

Austin heard Sam chuckling over there.

"Yep, fair enough," Sam said.

A few moments of silence followed.

"But what do you need the money for?" Sam asked. "Yacht, hookers, Ibiza?"

"No."

"Hmm . . . for me, yes."

Now Austin laughed a bit. But instantly became sorrowful. "My daughter is in a wheelchair."

Sam snapped his head around. "Oh . . . God . . . What happened?"

# Chapter 9

"What?"

"Believe me, we are doing everything we can . . ."

"You . . . you cannot be serious."

"I'm terribly sorry, sir. There are still numerous tests we need to run to be able to say more. Because, as of this moment, we can't really tell what could cause this. It is very unfortunate. I'm very sorry."

"And . . . what kind of infection? A virus or . . .?"

"It appears to be a very infectious bacteria that attacked her system, and because of her weak immune system, her body couldn't fight back properly, and . . . that's how it could cause such severe damage in the spine."

"No, I don't believe some disease is going to put my daughter in a wheelchair for a life!! She didn't have an accident, didn't break her spine, for God's sake!!"

"That's right, sir, and I repeat, it's too early to say anything, but . . . based on what we know so far, unfortunately . . . there's a significant and very real chance that the paralysis is not reversible."

Austin and his family's life turned into a nightmare. Questions left unanswered; nights spent sleepless.

The doctors were unable to tell the cause of infection for quite a long while. They were just guessing, mostly relying on what Cynthia told them as they tried to identify the contact, the person who could unintentionally be responsible for Cynthia's disease. At first, it seemed that it was a food-related infection, but that turned out to be a dead end. Then they went through numerous objects—clothing, headphones, cutlery—any and all ordinary things that Cynthia had come in contact with, none of which were considered by the doctors to be a likely culprit. And they were right. Until eventually, one of the most improbable ideas became a possible cause and finally was named as the one and only explanation. Everyone around Cynthia was reluctant to accept that this was actually happening to her.

\*\*\*

Cynthia was trying to comfort her friend, but it was utterly hopeless. She did regret not coming up with an ordinary explanation of how she got infected. The girl was sobbing on the edge of her bed so bitterly that Cynthia's reaction to this terrible news seemed casual.

"Just stop it, please! It wasn't your fault! I took it!" Cynthia said.

"But I should've told you."

"How could you have known? Nobody could. It's hard to believe, even for the doctors."

"Still. It's me . . . me . . ."

Cynthia had to realize that her friend would remain inconsolable until Cynthia could get out of the wheelchair and stand on her feet again.

# Chapter 10

"A makeup brush? A fuckin' makeup brush??" Sam said.

"Yes."

"Bullshit!"

"It's the truth."

"I don't believe it."

"Why would I lie about it?"

"Don't know. To arouse sympathy, to make me feel bad for you."

"Huh, because that would work with you just fine," Austin mocked. "But even if I was trying to do that, don't you think I'd just make it a simple car accident? Why would I make up such an absurdity?"

The only reason Austin dared to tell all this to Sam was because the story had never made it to any women's magazine or anywhere else as an article about a teenage girl's tragedy with cosmetology. So, since the story had never been published, besides in medical journals, Austin figured this would never lead back to him.

"Yeah, okay, that's fair, but still . . . a makeup brush is not like a syringe. How the hell could you get such a thing from it?"

"We all asked this question when we found out. Actually, we are still asking it. The doctor told us first."

"But how?"

"One of her friends had it on her face. It's called Staphylococcus. Nobody knew it was that easy to transmit, even the doctors were just shooting in the fucking dark for a long time."

"Jesus!" Sam was horrified. It took him some doing to take in what he just heard. "So, it's your daughter's recovery you need the money for."

Austin used a nod for an answer instead of words, not thinking how useless this was. But words came shortly after.

"According to the doctors, there's a treatment that could give her a good chance to walk again. It's just fucking expensive. I tried to take a loan, but I'm already up to my neck in debts so I couldn't. My girlfriend has way better credit, but seeing how much the whole treatment would cost, that amount is too big even for the two of us."

Austin fell into such a melancholic state while talking that he even forgot his current situation.

"And isn't there like a rich relative, a friend or someone you can turn to?"

"That rich, no. The ones I tried knew that would be money they would probably never see again in this lifetime, so all I got were sorrys and sympathies everywhere."

"Well . . . I understand, trust me. I'm reluctant to say this, but if I were you and I saw no other way, I wouldn't shy away from even dirtier business."

*Who's trying to arouse sympathy now?* "I have no doubt about that."

What Sam meant by "dirtier business" was not something Austin tried to find out, nor something Sam intended to detail. But it is odd how making ourselves look worse can often be the most efficient way of gathering sympathy.

"Although, kinda makes me curious what answer you cooked up to the question, 'Where did the money come from?" Sam said.

"Don't worry. I have a relatively acceptable explanation."

"Great. All my worries are gone now," Sam mocked, then flooded his gullet again.

Austin wasn't exaggerating when he called his explanation "relatively acceptable." If close family and friends were to ask about the money, they would be informed about the bank loan via an unnamed good friend because Austin knew he better not brush them off. As for the law angle to this thing, he unsuccessfully had tried to imagine a person so malicious that they would rat him out to the IRS after seeing his wheelchaired-daughter's recovery expenses. Jessica, Austin's girlfriend, supported him in everything, but even she had bought the wealthy-old-friend version. Austin hadn't paid much attention yet to working out the payback details and all the other little trifles. And he didn't intend to start caring about that until the minute he'd get his hands on the money that could give his daughter a chance.

"But getting back to today," Sam continued, "how did you know I have a safe in this house and it's not just for coupons or something?"

*The same way, I know about your gun, too.* "Do I need to repeat myself?" Austin asked, referring to his earlier stated lack of interest in sharing too much.

"No, not at all." *Worth a try.*

Austin remained silent about his journey leading up to now and the "where is the money from" explanation, and he did not fancy sharing anything about the source of his information either. Mentioning Sam's lil' brother, who is notoriously unable to shush his mouth when intoxicated during corporate events, wouldn't contribute much to his cause tonight. Nor to Sam's. To top it off, if on the off chance, they made it out alive tonight, he could bring some more trouble on himself by not keeping his mouth shut now.

"But honestly, I have no idea, what could make one do such a thing," Sam continued in a slightly theatrical tone. "Shoot dead, rob . . . Okay, I'm not particularly famous for being an angel, but I haven't really roughed up anyone too badly. So, all I can think of is that it was something very personal that has nothing to do with money or a job, and definitely a misunderstanding because—"

"You can stop there, I won't—"

"I didn't ask you a question just now!" Sam silenced Austin. "Just talking to myself. I hope, I'm allowed. You don't need to comment on anything. And if you don't like it, there's the door."

Austin got the message. Although he knew he couldn't keep his thoughts inside for too long, he joined Sam in the theater play.

"Why would anyone wanna rob a rich douchebag?" Austin asked. "I don't think it needs explanation. But who'd wanna kill? I gotta agree with your comment before—it has to be something very personal. Which I got no clue about. Luckily, I don't care. But if someone lives, the way . . . some people live, they shouldn't waste much time head scratching and wondering how come they have enemies."

"What the hell you mean?"

"I like talking to myself, too."

Sam stayed quiet.

"How classy—bankrupting our own companies and creating new ones," Austin said. "Sometimes overnight. I guess that's why these companies are called phoenix."

"Must've been smart-ass, whoever named it, huh?"

"All the assets and shit to transfer underpriced, or whatever, and piss on the employees. It's from so high above, you don't even see how many people you're drenching. I get the rebirth parallel, but still, I think these people should be called vultures . . . Oh, no, wait. I don't mean to offend vultures. They only benefit from death, but are not responsible for it . . . My apologies to them all."

"I see. A disgruntled ex-employee. I knew it."

"It could be but doesn't have to be."

"Then maybe one of your buddies complained about the big, bad boss man?" Sam felt something had clicked with the guy, so he tried to use that to extract more info out of him. "Some lowlifes got no clue how the system works and wouldn't last a day in the fields, even though some people do make it and then the lowlifes blame those people for their own failures."

"To understand what kind of person you are," Austin said, "there's no need for detectives or confidential sources. Anyone who ever worked for a guy like you, or simply browsed your name, can get the picture. All the shit you buy, anything you're spending money on, its real cost is always paid by others, right? That's why it's so easy and you don't feel its weight."

"Ah, okay, a vigilante," Sam said. "Some discount Robin Hood? Why don't you say that? Don't preach about your poor daughter. Just say whatever money you take from here tonight, tomorrow will feed those I ruthlessly ran over."

Austin ignored Sam's insult. "To be frank, I wonder how come you had only two guests tonight and there was no queue outside."

Both of them had evolved to the point where humor served as a distraction from their current predicament.

# Chapter 11

The gentlemen slowly chilled, and soon, they continued talking in a way calmer tone, as if they were less worried about how time-critical their situation was.

"My plan was to threaten you that I'll be watching you, and if you go to the police, I'll kill you. But if you let it go, it's over, and you'll never hear from me ever again," Austin explained.

"Nice."

"Not that it matters now, but . . . Do you think it would've worked?"

"We might still find out."

"Nah. Whatever happens, threatening is no longer an option even if I wanted it to be. Wouldn't seem too believable after all this."

"Well, that's actually true."

From time to time, Sam glanced at the laptop screen, hoping the internet was back, but it wasn't.

"If you don't mind, I'd like to ask you something else," Sam said, "and I think you can answer it."

"What?"

"How'd you get in?'

"Door was open."

"I doubt that."

"What a surprise. Put it next to the rest I've told you so far."

"You don't understand. I locked it. With the key."

"You sure?"

"Yeah, I'm sure."

"Well, then the guy who shot you has a key."

"Ah, so somehow you got a copy of my keys," Sam said, turning Austin's sentence against him.

"Not me."

"How?"

"I said, not me!" Austin stressed. "But even if I did, you should know by now I wouldn't tell you."

"You're uneasy, but you're slowly opening up, so we never know."

Austin got an idea. "Listen. When you got shot . . . do you remember—was the bang loud?"

"What?"

"The sound of the shot."

"I get it. It's just the dumbest question so far tonight. And honestly, I don't know. It was one moment, and I wasn't really worried about the sound. But . . . I think it wasn't that loud."

"Okay, this lines up with me hearing nothing from the outside."

"What are you talking about?"

"Silencer. As much I could work out the silhouettes, the other gun seemed too long. It must have a silencer."

"And why's that important? If you threw me a gun without a silencer now, wouldn't prove a thing. Plus, you have no intention of doing such a thing, so I don't see how it's supposed to help us."

"True." Austin accepted it sorrowfully. "But speaking of which, you might wanna start thinking about who—" Austin bit the sentence halfway through.

He wanted to ask Sam about who could have a key to this house. But he'd realized that trying to work out the shooter's identity—openly and out loud—could backfire. If the gunman were here listening, this might inspire him to act.

"Anyway," Sam said, "just to let you know, whatever I said, I believe you about your daughter."

"Don't bother, we're both fine not believing each other."

"Still. I don't have kids. But I guess, you already know that. My wife and I were trying for a long time, but it never happened. Even though we were told neither of us has a problem. They say stressed-out lifestyle—what the hell? In school, you casually hump your gal, straight away—conceives. Then, you treat your wife for months, and nothing. I couldn't have imagined this before."

"Neither could we," Austin said. "It took us like half a year trying. One month after that . . . never mind. So, it was after my wife switched to a much less stressful job."

"Insane, huh? It's sad, we're fighting a lot over this."

Sam was rolling the bottle in his hand; the hand gripping the gun was resting on his lap; his eyes and the gun barrel were constantly pointed straight at the doors. Soon though, he was vacantly staring at the floor, and his eyes closed. But after a few moments, he shook himself, cursing for almost drifting off, and resumed his watch.

Meantime, he couldn't get rid of the excruciating thought that he was unable to see the full scope of what was happening. *If this guy is telling the truth about his daughter and the money*, Sam thought, *then logically, he is not the shooter.* In which case, the gun Sam had to worry about could be anywhere. Which led to further questions: Who wants to see him dead and why? What if someone simply hired the shooter whose identity isn't actually important?

# Chapter 12

Lindsey Louise Vaughn had been striding through the twenty-sixth year of her life when she celebrated her first wedding anniversary. It took place in May 2004, followed by nine more anniversaries with the same husband. However, she spent the last one with a different man, or more precisely, with her next husband. This wasn't a case of flagrant unfaithfulness, at least not in the practical meaning of the word. Lindsey and her husband had agreed in the spring that there was no point in continuing, but the divorce turned out to grow way messier and longer than any of the parties could have imagined or would have preferred it to be. By the time the state officially declared the couple divorced, it was July, and Lindsey was already organizing her next wedding with her new husband-to-be. The nuptials went down at the beginning of October. That's why the time that passed between her two marriages could be viewed as jaw-droppingly short when compared to the average. If any statistics existed somewhere about this. But only the dates appearing on certain documents revealed this obscenely brief period. What had happened between the people involved made the picture more palatable, to an extent. But reading the story of Lindsey's private life strictly in the language of numbers, it was clear that she hadn't spent a single year without a wedding anniversary since 2004, even though this time period covered two different marriages.

"There he is," Lindsey pointed toward the stairs with her champagne glass.

"Thought you'd never make it," Sam said as Dylan stepped up to them.

"I know, can't believe I missed the speeches," Dylan mocked while peeling off his overcoat.

"Neither can I," Sam said, delivering a bit of sarcasm.

Lindsey preferred to join the ladies, who'd gathered by the piano, while the men engaged in conversation. Dylan Romeo Jackson wasn't a particularly close friend of Sam's, but their paths were linked in numerous ways, especially in business life. What had brought them here tonight was a tremendous party held for the occasion of a mutual friend's fiftieth birthday.

The restaurant itself was exceptionally charming and imposing, but the venue's primary booster and most inviting part was the group of adjoining rooms in the basement. Tailoring, clothing, accessories, and a beauty salon could all be found there. But the group leader and the largest room of all was the Piano Lounge. The Piano Lounge was plush and decorated to the nines, with very expensive abstract artwork on the walls, decorative furniture not suited for sitting, and real fur rugs, which were rolled up and put aside in the corner during events. In that same corner, a beautiful grand piano, the room's title character, stood. Guests who were qualified to play on it were allowed to do so, as long as they maintained the level of respect that such a sophisticated instrument deserved.

Despite the inconceivably high prices of the interior decor items, drinks were quite affordable. Yet, Sam and Dylan didn't see this as an invitation for binge drinking. Even though, most of the party guests seemed to disagree. None of them have anything against such a thing; they simply weren't in the mood. It's probably because none of them were particularly thrilled to be here tonight.

"Look, I really don't wanna bother you with this, but you know, I'm on a deadline, so if—"

"Yeah, yeah, of course, I didn't forget. I'm just a tad preoccupied these days."

"I know, and I'm sorry. If you can't fit it in, then—"

"No, no, we can do it. Today, I actually made my next Wednesday evening free. So to say."

"That's great. It would still be in time."

"The only thing, I'll spend the evening on the mountain, so if Skype's okay, then we got no problem."

"That's perfect, we don't need to meet. All I need is your experience and razor-sharp brain, the rest can be anywhere."

"Good."

"So you're saying, on Wednesday you're going to be out there in your little bunker, for sure?"

"Yep."

The music was hellishly loud, just as it was supposed to be. The bar was set up across from the piano, and the DJ stand was in the middle by the wall. Everything had its place, and various nooks and corners featured different themes. Some were buzzing from grand explanations about how our world works. Others hosted tipsy poster girls who were tearing up on each other's shoulders, and a few, of course, were occupied with tongue tangling and the exchanging of phone numbers. The dance floor in front of the DJ stand was prickly from the remains of broken glasses, sticky from spilled drinks, and vastly entertaining due to the abandonment of dignity all over the place.

Sam and Dylan moved around the dance floor to the toilet corridor to chat. It was the farthest they could get from the speakers. No congestion had formed in the corridor, however, the traffic wasn't negligible.

"How you doin' with Lindsey?" Dylan asked.

"Huh, what you think?" Sam replied, lifting his glass to his mouth.

"Well, if you're just half as good as you look, that's already much better than my first marriage."

"What? We're not pretending shit!"

"Uh, maybe I never told you about my first marriage?"

They both burst out in moderate laughs, then Dylan took over the talking. But somewhere in the middle of listening, Sam got distracted. What struck his eye was the staff toilet, which was the farthest one away from him. This wasn't the first big event Sam had attended in this very restaurant, and he was aware that the huge number of attendees tended to reduce the significance of the signs on the restroom doors. All of them were unisex anyway, but the staff's and guests', including the one for disabled were separate. But at an event this size, guests used the staff's, just as the staff used the guests', none of which ever led to differences of opinion or dissatisfaction.

Something similar had caught Sam's attention, although it had a slightly different nature. A waiter had just stepped out of the staff toilet when a guest moved in to claim the vacant room. But the guest happened to encounter an unforeseen obstacle. The door's closing mechanism was just about to fully close the door when the unsuspecting guest hit the handle at the same time, and the door locked again. The surprised guest looked like he even forgot about his own urgency for a few seconds. But before he began to engage in unbridled conjecture, another restroom freed up. And as luck would have it, there was nobody else waiting, so he locked himself in to do his business.

Sam couldn't help but smile, a smile wider than any induced by other jokes that day.

"What're you grinning for?" Dylan asked.

"Uh, nothing, sorry, I just got distracted. Go on."

Dylan was just about to pick up right where he had left off when Sam interrupted.

"You know what? Actually . . ." Sam went on to share what had happened moments ago, which sent the conversation in a totally new direction and drowned the unfinished topic into oblivion, at least temporarily.

In the meantime, Sam kept an eye on the most interesting door without making their chat lose momentum. After a few minutes passed, the obvious was confirmed—the black-shirted bartender slipped out wearing the most innocent face that ever appeared in this world.

Sam was hit by a small rush of nostalgia. Usually, at grand-scale parties such as this, the guests and even the staff assisted their evening with a certain type of hit. Sam had used the bathroom for the second time maybe fifteen minutes ago, and the top of the little, black table adjacent to the toilet had seemed a bit whiter compared to his previous visit.

"By the way, have you seen my brother?" Sam asked. "He must have come way before me."

"He did. I kinda lost track of him for like an hour. He's probably smooth talking with the big heads somewhere. You might wanna keep an eye on him."

"Nah, can't make bigger damage than what he does at work."

"Don't be so sure," Dylan replied. "You know, he can't hardly stop his mouth, especially when he's drinking."

"We grew up together, same schools, and I even made a spot for him at the company. Please tell me more because I really had no chance to know him."

"Okay, fine, all's I'm sayin', it wouldn't be so cool if he jawed something he shouldn't to them."

"What can I do?" Sam said with his arms wide open. "Sew up his mouth? Lock him away?"

"You know, I've seen him talking drunk to strangers in bars."

"So did I, trust me. And I shared my full-fledged opinion with him the next morning."

"Don't care if he was bragging over his drug stories. And you know what? Not even the stories about his married brother's sluts."

"Quiet, you dumb shit!" Sam was fuming.

"Chill, no one's here!" Dylan silenced him. "Point being, bro, we both know that your dirty nighttime adventures aren't the worst thing about you he could make public."

# Chapter 13

The bottle was rolling in his hand, his head was spinning on his neck. Hard as he tried, he fell short of thinking of someone he knew who could do this to him or even be a part of it. Not deliberately, at least. His younger brother, Kevin, was a real mess, and no doubt he'd inherit everything built by Sam if Sam were dead. But Sam doubted he could do something like this. Even if he'd delivered a certain amount of assistance to someone in tonight's assault, it must have only been by using his big mouth. Sam vowed to question him thoroughly—if he survived all this.

And then there was Dylan. No way he had anything to do with this. They'd been friends for almost two decades, ever since Dylan had that bar fight with a few local scumbags who had provoked him for his skin color. Not to mention the Skype chat that provided him with the most solid alibi on earth. But despite all this, or perhaps because of this, an absurd thought nested itself into Sam's head. The fact that he had a bullet planted in his back made it obvious that someone wanted him dead. And essentially, since everyone belonged to the group of people above suspicion, the one responsible for this must necessarily be among them. Except, if the one behind this would profit hugely from his death, and they had never had the pleasure of meeting in person. For a fact, individuals who fit into this category could possibly be many.

"Look, man . . . soon, it's gonna be time to decide whether to believe me or not." Austin sent a few words to the large room. "We can't sit here 'til morning."

A great many of Sam's thoughts were indeed revolving around this very decision. He kept running and checking the facts in his mind over and over again. Everything that'd been said so far, how much sense certain things made, and so on. Including the makeup-brush story. That was so hair-raising that if someone came up with it under circumstances like this, then it had to be true. But even if it was, that still did not guarantee that this guy had no intention of killing him at all. What if he had come equipped to open the safe by force? If he knew about it, which he did, he might also have known that it was a quality safe, but you didn't need to hire Ocean's gang to gain access to its content. To have the owner open it would certainly make more sense. But he was not in the other one's shoes, not thinking with that guy's head. So that small percentage of chance would be reserved for this option.

"Agree," Sam said. "But I still pass. You might say the truth."

Then something else occurred to Sam. Didn't the guy share way too much with him? He had said that he didn't want to say anything about himself, but basically within the same breath, he told his daughter's story. Isn't this whole infection thing rare enough to give a sufficient lead to the police? Based on his statement, they could search all the hospitals looking for a similar case and could easily track the man down.

Maybe he hadn't been too shy to tell Sam all that stuff because he was counting on Sam to not survive the night. Or simply just forgot himself and got carried away. Could be. Or he believes that everything he said is not enough for the police to find him. In case of the last one, he might be very right. Sam had already forgotten the name of this Staphi something bacterium.

This thought disappeared quickly in favor of a far more important one—he needed his cell phone. No debate. Even though every step he would take toward it would risk another bullet. The guy was also right about that. If Sam didn't believe him, he could have made the walk a while ago. But if he did venture out, either to grab his phone or to switch the router back on, both required him to give up his current "foxhole." It might not be the safest place to hide, but the chances of his body getting decorated with further bullet holes were significantly lower there than anywhere else.

But if he were to come out, the end could catch up with him anywhere in the house, anytime. It would take nothing more than a look in the wrong direction at the wrong moment or reacting slower than the other. That's all and that's it. But it might be worth a try. Testing the other one's word. But Sam figured only a fool would take that risk just to test a stranger's word. No, if someone had to move, it better be the other guy.

"But I truly agree that we cannot sit here forever," Sam said.

"No, we can't."

"Not me for sure, at least. If I don't get medical help, sooner or later I'm gonna bleed out. So even if you don't wanna risk more than necessary, you still gotta move your ass. Because if I feel like I'm running out of time, then I'll start shooting and then we'll see what happens. Understand what I'm saying?"

"Yes."

"Great."

Sam was aware that this little speech could come back at him, but he figured there wasn't much worth waiting for. He was increasingly feeling colder and weaker. Soon, he would run out of time.

*He just said, he's afraid to risk, and now he's threatening me with a shoot-out?* Austin thought.

Austin's silence had taken a toll on Sam's confidence.

"Don't get me wrong," Sam tried again. "I really wanna avoid anybody starting to shoot in my house, but . . . if that happens . . . I guarantee, I will fire every last round from the mag before I punch the clock."

Austin knew there was one absolute solution to advance their situation. If he put down his gun and walked into the room in front of Sam with his hands above his head, he'd likely earn Sam's trust. But the picture of himself standing defenseless in front of a man with a gun in his hand and a bullet in his back . . . well. Not to mention the big unknown— the other gunman's whereabouts.

"You thinking what to do now, right?"

"Yeah."

"Me, too."

A short silence followed.

"You ever heard about the ship called *Endurance*?" Sam asked out of the blue.

"No."

"An explorer from the 1910s."

"Aha," Austin said. He had no idea where Sam was going with this.

"I never liked history, but hell, it did stick."

"An explorer, in history class?"

"Geography then, whatever. Who cares?"

"Okay, what about it?"

"This guy called Shackleton thought he was gonna be the first one to ever cross Antarctica. I guess he wanted to do something since he missed out to be the one to discover it. But his little expedition kinda went off-road."

"What? Crossing Antarctica with a ship?"

"No, he just wanted to come ashore with the ship."

"I see."

"So, in the fall of 1914, they left from Argentina and the sea voyage was already fucked. Struggled for weeks, dragging in the rough weather until the point when the ship froze in the sea."

"That's steep."

"Well, they went to Antarctica; they obviously prepared for everything. Except for "ice and cold." Sam chuckled, which sent a sharp pain down his back, so he cut it off. "They were waiting for the weather to get better, but that never happened. The crew had to abandon the ship and set out on foot with much worse chances than were calculated in the first place. And the hull crushed under the weight of the ice and sunk slowly within the course of weeks."

"If I'm not mistaken, other ships had issues with ice back then too."

"Yeah. But all of those people made it, at least. Although, the world war almost had come to its end before they saw land. Bit of a stretch, of course. But they survived."

"Astonishing story, but what's that got to do with anything?"

"Inaction increases pressure, buddy. Not that the ship encapsulated in ice had any kind of choice, but pressure, given enough time, overcomes anything. Nothing can stand against it. Sooner or later, everything snaps underneath."

Austin received the message.

"If now we don't risk less, later we will have to risk more, then it will have to be all."

"Then go ahead!" Austin flared up. "Get up from there and do the look around!"

"Told you already. I'm storing a bullet in my back, so if someone's to be more cautious here, it's gonna be me."

"That's why you have more to lose," Austin replied. "Your time runs out sooner. You said something like that too."

Sam realized that the guy had a point. Yet, he tried to make him move first.

"True . . . But, if we have to wrap it up with a shootout, that's hardly gonna do any good for us. One of us might live, but nothing guaranteed. My offer's still in place. If you accept, we both can end up good. You wanna earn my trust? A cell phone is the price. And I pay you back with what's in the safe. If you told the truth and it really isn't you who wants to kill me, then go to my car and bring me my phone. And I open the safe for you. That's it."

"What makes you think I wouldn't drive away?"

"Well, you can do that. But it would be extremely awkward for you if I somehow survived."

# Chapter 14

Austin couldn't believe the night had deteriorated so bad, and he was in such trouble. The number of banana peels it took to slip this far. The dreadful realization clawed its way up to the surface again: if he had hidden in the large room, he might have figured something out with Sam, and this might all be over by now. But even that was dwarfed by the more painful thought that if only he had taken a few different steps when he had first entered the house, everything would've turned out differently. If he'd spotted the gunman from the entrance side of the corridor, he wouldn't have pulled back to the living room in terror. He'd have gone straight out the door. That's all he would've needed. Then he could've disappeared among the trees, and he'd probably still be running somewhere down toward the city. As long as his daughter was alive, he would never have given up hoping, and tonight's casualties would only have been the bucks he spent on the gun.

But even though he had seen the gunman late, the night could still have played out differently. If in the very second that his brain chose the living room, he had gone the other way, then what would've happened next would still have been better. Even if he had made some noise on his way out, he would likely have had the lead, and he could've hopped the railing, run up the slope, crossed the road, and vanished in the woods. Even with the knowledge that someone had been in the house, the gunman wouldn't have had a chance to track him down. Getting lost in the dark and not crossing his own doorstep until morning wouldn't have been a problem. Instead, he could easily be about to meet death now.

"Cover yourself from each way." Sam was trying to encourage Austin in preparation. "For me, you can even shoot to where you think the other one is. Just bring me my phone in one piece."

"Alright."

Sam removed the car key from his pocket and launched it with great momentum toward the sliding door, aiming where the green Tanqueray bottle had come from.

Austin heard the tiny metal-plastic piece slide along the floor, slow down, and stop about a foot and a half away from the kitchen island.

"Where is it in the car?"

"I don't know. But it's there."

"How's that?"

"I was on the phone the whole way. If you were driving behind me close enough, you could've seen for yourself. I hung up just about before I got onto the mountain road. I think it slipped out of my suit pocket."

"And you didn't notice?"

"Don't tell the cops, but when I'm driving in a suit, I never strap in. But today I chose the belt and put the suit jacket on the passenger seat. When I got out, I didn't check if the phone was still in the pocket, so it must be in the car."

"What if it fell out after?"

"Where? On the roof, the stairs? I would've heard that. No, it's on the seat, or under. But sure, it's there."

"Yeah, by elimination, right?"

"Fine, leave it, then! Just throw the key back and don't go anywhere!" Sam was fed up.

"Not saying I won't go."

"Then shut up and go! And you better hurry. Besides, if it turns out it's somewhere between the car and the front door, at least it will shorten the trip."

It occurred to Austin that if they weren't in such a pickle right now, he would probably be entertained by Sam's dark humor. After a proper look around, he leaned forward and took the key.

"Alright," he said. "You just sit tight over there . . . drink and . . . stay alive. I need some time out there. Just . . . just leave me a little. Okay?"

"Sure, take it easy. Keep your shit together. And I take the advice, all of it." As if on cue, Sam removed another ounce from the green bottle.

Meantime, a storm was rising in Austin's head. Thoughts and doubts were fighting to overcome each other. One of the strongest was how to make it through the corridor. Austin figured that if the gunman were here in the house, he must have heard them talking about the plan. That would mean confrontation was inevitable since the gunman obviously couldn't afford to let them retrieve Sam's cell phone and call for help. So, if the gunman were in the house and Austin came out from behind the kitchen island, he'd certainly walk into a gunfight.

The settling debris of the storm was building a thick layer in Austin's head. *Look at it the other way*, Austin told himself. If the shooter was lurking somewhere outside, then he'd be back where he started—he could get shot from anywhere. But Austin figured there was a lower chance of that. From the gunman's perspective, it would be quite a risk to have left the house knowing the two of them were stuck in there. From the outside, the guy couldn't be sure they wouldn't come to some kind of agreement inside, which might include calling help via the internet. No, Austin concluded, unless the shooter took the router outside under his armpit, he must still be in here.

Austin's head filled up with options; almost everything seemed imaginable. Except one thing— lasting much longer sitting on the kitchen floor in here. He had to try. His situation wouldn't get any better with an hour passing. Neither would Sam's. And if Sam really meant what he'd said earlier, and he feels the end closing in on him, he might really get up and go to the car himself, sparing no one he finds in his way.

Of course, the shorter way led through the corridor. If Austin failed to convince himself to get going, this would be the other option: wait patiently since Sam's condition was getting worse. If Sam were to make it to the "screw it" state of mind and went to get his phone, the kitchen would not be on his way. And then Sam himself could settle things with his attacker, in here or out there. Although the huge problem with this was that it would only serve to confirm Sam's theory that Austin alone had attacked him, and to avoid gunfire, he was waiting for Sam to bleed out. And unfortunately, it's pretty hard to deny something when every move we make does nothing but confirm that. And then, why wouldn't Sam start with the kitchen, trying to eliminate the only assumed attacker in order to make the phone call without being disturbed?

Austin began to snap. His eyes were getting wet. He had to pull the hat off his face because he could barely breathe. Whatever option he chose, he couldn't dodge the gunfight. His only hope was that there were indeed only two in the house. The vanished internet connection, however, seemed to prove that wrong. The gunman wouldn't have left Sam behind if Sam had returned to consciousness. And if the gunman had left before Sam woke up, then what had happened to the internet? He felt like he was never going to run out of questions. Unlike time.

Austin noticed a kitchen towel roll sitting on the counter not far from the sink. The idea was born instantly. Austin looked around, grabbed the roll, and ripped off one sheet. From his pocket, he took out a ballpoint pen that he'd left in his jacket that morning. It wrote surprisingly well on the uneven, two-ply paper towel, and thanks to its absorbent nature, it didn't smear.

He kept looking up above his head from the paper, after every few words. When he finished, he wiped his eyes, folded the paper and slipped it into the inner pocket of his jacket.

*So be it!*

# Chapter 15

The Ruger was mildly vibrating. It had no chance of doing otherwise in the shaking hand holding it. Close alongside the corridor's wall, Austin was approaching the arched opening. He was worried he could pass out at any moment. Since Sam had indicated that he wouldn't mind, Austin was earnestly considering blindly releasing a few bullets into the dark corridor. But after a deep breath, he poked his head out from behind the wall for a fraction of a second, just long enough to allow his left eye to catch a brief glimpse of the corridor.

He saw nobody. He waited a bit, took a few more deep breaths, and looked out again, this time for a little longer. Not much light wound up in the corridor, but it was just enough to leave no corner utterly dark, allowing Austin to check every square foot. Completely empty, no one around. Austin threw himself away from the wall, across the turn and toward the entrance. Halfway, he stopped and spun around. No figure came at him from anywhere. No shots were fired.

Austin carefully opened the front door and looked to his right, up the stairs leading to the roof. It was all clear too. He looked around into the dark night in all directions and back behind himself into the house. Still nobody, only him. He stepped out onto the small, forty-square-foot terrace.

He had made it out of the house. There was cool, fresh air to breathe again, but he was nowhere near to true relief yet.

From the moment he stepped onto the first step of the stairs to the roof, Austin was concealed by the second external wall. There were only two ways to look—up and down the stairs. But they also were the only two ways out. He was protected and trapped at the same time, inside the stairwell. Although, he pretty much was his kitchen hideout, too. Keeping his back up against the wall of the house, Austin moved sideways up the stairs, turning his head back and forth as he went, checking for the shooter up and down the stairs. He had only two steps left before he reached the roof when he realized a missed opportunity and stopped. He had been so preoccupied watching out for the shooter in the corridor that he had not checked the router's condition. But this very question departed Austin's head the same way it had come in: with lightning speed. He was here, now, on the stairs, and he had to make it to the car.

He squatted behind the wall as he got on the rooftop, peered over the wall, and scanned the parking area. It appeared that nobody was waiting for him. The only thing in the parking area was Sam's car, looking quite lonely but unharmed. Austin was coming to the conclusion that if the gunman were still here, he was not inside the house. Otherwise, he wouldn't have let Austin out so easily and risked that Austin would leave Sam behind and flee. If that were true, then the gunman must be either here, waiting for his moment to strike, or he did indeed leave in the very beginning, however unlikely. Maybe the gunman had never seen Austin at all. Or even if he did, maybe he heard the "we go separate ways" monologue and figured Sam was dead. And maybe he figured that leaving a witness behind would not be such a big problem since it seemed like the witness had also broken into the house. If neither the gunman nor the witness had seen the other's face, then the police could equally get to the one who didn't pull the trigger. And if the shooter was thinking this way, then Austin had spent all this time hiding in the kitchen for absolutely no reason. But it still was just a big maybe.

Instead of the many and dizzying possibilities, Austin needed to focus on getting to the car, finding the phone, and making his way back down the stairs with the phone in his hand. As Sam had said, that was the price of believing that Austin had nothing to do with the bullet in his back.

What's more, if all of this were to come to pass, they could even celebrate their luck together, since it would mean that the gunman was assuming Sam was dead and had left a long time ago. Then, Austin could quickly empty the safe, Sam could call for help, and they would part ways. That would be it. Sam's priority would obviously be to catch his real attacker, and the police wouldn't even have to be informed about the other dumbass and the contents of the safe. In theory. Too bad this plan wasn't resting on legs as stable as the massive pillars under the concrete house.

Austin started to move toward the car in a crouching position alongside the waist-high wall. Sam hadn't driven onto the roof with both axles, so the car was parked half on the bridge, which meant a few yards of open space between the wall and the car. Austin did not welcome it at all because he would be exposed but he had no choice. Before leaving the wall, he got down on the ground and looked underneath the car. Clear. He looked around once again, pointed the key in his left hand toward the car, and pressed the red button.

\*\*\*

"Hey! Are you still here?"

Austin had crept across the house so quietly that Sam hadn't heard him leaving at all. For obvious reasons, Austin had not cued Sam in by yelling, "I'm leaving now!"

"You hear me? You still there?" Sam called out to Austin again, but still, no reply. Then, a very familiar sound hit his ear—the double beep of his car unlocking.

*Shit, he made it out!* Sam felt dizzy. It was mild but escalating. He quickly thought through the current situation. No room for hesitation any longer. He stood up behind the sofa and got going.

While pointing his gun steadily forward where his eyes were scanning, he made it to the closest door. It led to the corridor and had been left ajar, so Sam didn't step in front of it. Instead, he slowly stretched out his left arm to reach the handle, making sure the rest of his body stayed covered by the wall. Lacing his fingers around the handle, he opened the door all the way, took a deep breath, and looked out into the corridor. It was empty. He stepped into the corridor, which was now well lit, as Sam had left the door open, and looked down at the router. There were no lights on, neither green nor red. Sam stepped silently down the corridor and slowly entered the small, windowless bedroom. He saw no company in there either. Slowly, he approached the closets and opened them one by one. Only clothes inside, folded or hung.

He paused for a moment and caught a breath. He glanced at the bed which looked so inviting. But he resisted the temptation. Instead, he rushed to the socket next to the bed and snatched his phone out of the charger.

# Chapter 16

Austin was scouring the area in a squat as he pressed his back up against the rear, driver's side door of Sam's car. He scanned what he could see of the narrow road, trees, and bushes. Then he gently opened the driver's door and inspected the front seats and straight after, the floor. There was no phone.

Panic took over. Austin spun around. But still, nothing suspicious. He recalled what Sam had said about the last time he had his phone with him, and how it must've slipped out of his suit pocket on the passenger seat. It must be somewhere there. He climbed inside the car and checked everything again, more thoroughly this time: the front seats, in between and by the door, the floor. He even looked inside the glove compartment, checked the dashboard and the visor. Nothing. Then he searched the back of the car: seats, between and under, the floor and the rear shelf. Everything. Sam's cell phone was nowhere.

*God damn it!*

A terrible thought made its way inside him, and it was painful in a way that a bullet never could be—Sam had played him! Austin quickly climbed out of the car and closed the door without re-activating the central locking system. If Sam had fooled him, there was only one reason— calling for help from inside. What else for? His phone must be somewhere in the house. Which means Sam had never believed a single word that he said.

Austin imagined police vehicles blocking the road that led off the mountain and cops searching the perimeter with lights and dogs. He had no idea of the probability of this scenario or how fast this could all happen. The image in his head was more vivid than the landscape in front of him. He had to go back to clear the air with Sam. If he fled now, he might eventually face serious repercussions. The police would hunt for him. Plus, Sam wasn't some average dude; he was rich and influential. Who knows how that would affect the police? Who knows what kind of resources they would mobilize in order to catch the guy who had assaulted Samuel Hayes? Also, choosing to run now would be a final farewell to the money, and if he were to get caught later, there would be no chance of clearing himself. He would march into prison as the fool who had taken the credit for someone else's crime because he arrived late to his own one.

No! He couldn't run. There still might be a way out—go back to the house and clear things up. The downside of this move, though, was that it would make him look like the real shooter, who came back to finish what he had left half done. Although, after all of this, only God followed Sam's line of thinking.

***

*"911, what's your emergency?"*

"There's an armed man in my house and he's trying to kill me! He shot me!"

Sam looked out to the corridor while he was giving his address. He could hear the operator typing intensely.

*"Right. What's your name, sir?"*

"Sam."

*"Where did you get shot, Sam?"*

"In my back."

*"Where are you now?"*

"Inside, in my house."

*"And where's the gunman?"*

"Up on the roof, but he can come back anytime."

*"Right. Are you alone in the house?"*

"Yes."

*"Can you get out safely?"*

"No, don't think so."

*"Can you hide somewhere?"*

"Uh . . . yes. I mean, I think I can hold him off. I have my own gun." Sam was watching the end of the corridor while slowly backing into the large room. "Just hurry! I'm getting dizzier and feel like I can pass out anytime."

*"I understand, sir. Help is on the way. Just try to get somewhere safe. If you can, lock yourself in a room or a closet but don't hang up. Stay with me. Okay?"*

"Okay, I think—"

"Sam!!"

The yell made Sam tremble. He'd made it inside the large room, and turned his back to the sofa. He aimed his gun at the corridor's far end, still holding the phone to his ear. Then he spotted a figure behind the kitchen's sliding door. But the shout had come from the far end of the corridor. Whoever the figure was in the kitchen, they couldn't have shouted Sam's name.

Sam and the figure made eye contact.

The popping sound was just as reduced, yet just as powerful, as the very same sound a couple of hours earlier. The bullet hit Sam's left shoulder. He staggered back from the power of the impact, and the phone spun out from his hand, flying across the room. As he fell to the floor, Sam opened fire toward the kitchen. The bullets blasted apart the glass in the sliding door, and ended their journey in the kitchen wall. The figure did not fire again and disappeared behind the wall of the corridor. The phone had broken apart, and the pieces wound up all over the room.

Sam's fall was softened by the edge of the sofa and the door. His brain refused to process the sensation of pain, and he kicked himself backwards the instant he hit the ground. Within seconds, he made it behind the sofa then crawled across it to his laptop, which was still lying there, the battery dead.

The figure on the kitchen side instantly realized the danger of standing in the open against the wall. He quickly threw himself behind the kitchen island, right to Austin's previous spot.

"What do you want?" Sam yelled at the top of his lungs. "What the fuck you want from me??"

The new bullet had triggered an adrenaline bomb in Sam's body, and a stabbing, burning pain was piercing his insides from head to toe. He was on his back, and the enormous pressure from his own weight was bearing down on his first bullet wound, raising his agony to a whole new, unbearable level.

"Anyone enters this room, I'm gonna gun the shit out of you!!" he cried out.

The few inches between the floor and the bottom of the sofa were just enough for Sam to see through to the doors and keep watch. He couldn't be seen behind the sofa, so whoever opened fire on him would be shooting blindly and could easily miss. Moreover, he had a clear shot under the sofa to the door, and a hit in the foot could make the other one collapse to the floor, making an easy target.

"Told you, there's someone else! Told you it wasn't me!!" Austin yelled from the corridor.

"What do you want? Why the fuck you wait so long, motherfucker?" Sam yelled back. "Say something, you piece of shit!"

"Why did you fuck me?" Austin shouted. "Your phone wasn't in the car. It wasn't anywhere. You got it. You got the phone. Right?"

Sam didn't answer.

"You called the police? Huh?"

"I don't know where the phone's at, I swear!"

"Don't lie, God damn it! You called the cops while I was out there??"

Sam hesitated to answer.

"No!" he said. "But don't matter, I'm gone soon, anyway. Bleeding out. But if you . . . if you swear you're not with him, then help me!"

"I'm done trying to convince you. You believe whatever you want."

"I believe you now! And that's why you gotta be with me! Two against one."

"Bullshit!"

"Listen! If you don't leave me here, then all this won't be for nothing. If you help me and I make it, you get all the money you need. Think about that! Think about your daughter!"

This tore Austin apart. Everything seemed to be skyrocketing. He'd spent pretty much all night contemplating his choices, but now each and every second became gravely important. And then, a thought just came out of nowhere. *Why's the other one still got his mouth shut? What's the point? He just gave away he's here.*

An explanation quickly formed in Austin's head.

"Why do you think this asshole still doesn't say a word?" Austin called out into the room.

"I don't know."

"Maybe because you'd recognize the voice."

Sam pondered this concept.

"Maybe . . . But if he gets away with this, we'll never know. Help me and it'll be good for both of us. I promise."

"He's lying!!" The shout cut through the air. "He called the police while you were outside!!"

Sam and Austin couldn't move from the shock, although for slightly different reasons. After a few seconds of silence, there was only one word Sam managed to squeeze out of his mouth.

"Lindsey?"

# Chapter 17

The Burgundy glasses didn't have much chance to dry out, as they were refilled constantly. The two friends were having a great time chatting and laughing and carrying on. But the cheerful mood eventually turned disconcertingly serious and straight out overwhelming, inevitable on occasions such as this.

"Whoa, honey, this . . . this is a little bit steep."

"You started."

"But not this, that . . . whatever."

"I am just talking about something you brought up. Don't know why you're scared."

"It's just . . . you seem like . . . "

"Like?"

"Like you're serious."

"What if I am?"

The two women had known each other since high school. They were very familiar with the various levels of each other's drunken behavior. That is why they couldn't decide who was more frightened hearing the other's words. But the more that vanished from the next bottle of red, the more evanescent the initial scare seemed.

"He's never been good to you."

"He was as good as he could."

"As much as he felt like! And that's not the same."

\*\*\*

Lindsey and Elizabeth didn't float this topic again for days. Next time not a single drop of alcohol was consumed, and neither was any at the occasions after that.

"Sure you want this?" Elizabeth asked.

"And you?" Lindsey replied.

"I wouldn't turn to anyone else with something like this. But you're the last person I'd want to put at risk."

"You mean without cutting someone else in?"

They both turned silent.

"Anyway, it's only a couple of hours, right?" Elizabeth said.

"Yes."

"Then we do what we discussed. I start something on Netflix and tag us on Face from your phone."

"Yeah. I was thinking about posting . . ."

"And?"

"Maybe we should scratch that in case something goes wrong."

"Like what?"

"Don't know, anything. If I get caught."

"Lin . . ."

"Or even if I get seen somewhere in the city," Lindsey continued, "then I can say later I had business there. But if at the same time you post from my phone at your place, that's . . . you understand."

"Fine . . . Fine, you're right."

"I don't know how deep they dig these cases, but I guess they can check anything. But they know it's easy to play with logins. So, I don't think they care too much."

"Yeah, but what if . . ."

"What?"

"How about ordering some food?"

"Good idea . . . Before, after?"

"I don't know."

"After I'm back, I think . . . And we make sure the delivery guy sees us both."

Lindsey and Elizabeth went through every single detail, factor, and potential trouble that they could possibly think of.

"What about communication?" Elizabeth asked.

"Texting only. Nothing incriminating."

"But we don't use our phones anyway, no?"

"No, of course not. I'll get a couple of old ones. Still . . ."

"Right"

"But first, you don't send anything, no matter what."

"But . . . what if you're not back for long? How will I know—"

"You send nothing," Lindsey impressed upon Elizabeth. "I text you if I see fit. Like: *I'm on my way* or *sorry, hon, I'm still stuck in here, gonna be late*, things like that."

Elizabeth nodded.

"We can even work out some kind of coded language or something. Ordinary messages, nothing suspicious. In case . . . I don't know, somebody checks it, I lose it, they steal it, whatever. Just to be sure.

"Alright," Elizabeth said. "But should we save a few random numbers in the phones."

"Why?"

"As you said; just to be sure. It's better if they're not empty, I guess. Ten or twelve will do."

"Okay."

"And how are you going to ditch the gun? Phone—easy, anywhere. But the gun . . ."

"The river would be the best. I could toss everything."

"You wanna make that detour? You know how many will see you?"

"They will anyway."

"No, not if I pick you up."

"You won't leave the house by any means, we agreed on that!"

"I know, but come on, by the time you get through the city—"

"I'll get a taxi."

"Uh, yeah, sure you will!"

"Fine, you're right," Lindsey said. "I can bury the gun out there. No one will find it."

Except what to watch on Netflix, they basically planned and worked out the entire evening down to the smallest of details. It seemed like they were prepared for everything and had left no room for surprises.

# Chapter 18

Lindsey gently turned the key and opened the door as quietly as she could. No sooner had she taken one step inside when she heard Sam pacing in the large room. His hard-soled shoes, which she had been upset about many times for leaving marks on the parquet, were turning out to be quite valuable to her.

This half of the house was totally dark. Lindsey stuck her head out from behind the wall into the corridor and saw that the door to the large room was ajar. She could hear her husband sitting down onto the swivel chair behind his desk. This was far from fortunate because now he was facing her, but the partially open door was blocking his view. She surely could sneak all the way to the door along the corridor's left side without being seen. She cautiously moved forward, each step slower than the one before. Her heart was racing, and as she got to the door, it pumped so hard against her chest that it felt like the kicks of an eight-month fetus. Then, she heard the sound of Sam's voice, and she froze.

"I'm here, you hear me?"

*"Yep, hear you, but crappy."*

"That's fine, won't get better. We can shout."

*"Well, you made me used to it."*

"So funny, ha ha. Let's hope we don't get disconnected completely, so you can do your shit all on your own."

*"No, no, all cool, man, let's kill it."*

"Thought so . . . But wait, let me pour myself one. I kinda feel like I'm gonna need some lubricant for this. I'll be back in a minute."

*"Sure."*

Lindsey stood fixed just outside his door. She could hear her husband getting up off his chair, and through the gap, she saw him walking to the kitchen. She quickly receded to the small, windowless bedroom, where she tried to analyze the situation and answer the very expensive and pressing question—should she shoot her husband while he's on a live video call?

If the guy on the other end of the call knew where Sam was, and likely he did, he would call the cops right away. It might even do if she were to kill Sam right now, while he was in the kitchen and out of the webcam's sight. But maybe the person on the call would hear something or would just grow suspicious about Sam being off the call for so long. Contemplating this option, Lindsey figured she could disconnect the internet, and she started thinking about the router. That surely would make Sam come out of the room to see what was going on, and then she could gun him down from the dark without a problem. That could work.

But there was a risk to that, too. If the chat got disrupted and Sam didn't call back, the other person would phone him. If Sam didn't pick up, that could lead to trouble. Lindsey, of course, knew that the internet around there wasn't the most reliable thing, and a disrupted connection would not likely be enough for anyone to call the police. But Sam not signing in again and not picking up the phone—that might be.

No, the smartest and safest way was to wait until they finished. If she waited it out quietly, it should not be a problem. The later Sam's body got discovered, the better.

If enough time were to pass, even she, the concerned wife, could be the one to find her husband's corpse.

Lindsey took a deep breath and waited.

***

*"Okay then, talk later. And thanks again!"*

"Yeah, yeah, fine, bye, goodnight!"

After her husband ended the call, Lindsey poked her head out of the bedroom into the corridor and listened. She heard Sam walking around and stretching. When the moving stopped, she stepped into the corridor and tiptoed to the door of the large room. From there, she could see the far side of the room. Sam was covered by the door, but telling by the silence, he was motionless. Lindsey gathered her courage and gently pushed the door open.

Sam was standing between his desk and the sofa, facing the balcony, a glass in his hand. Both of Lindsey's hands were shaking even though she was trying to steady them. She removed her finger from the trigger to be sure not to fire before it was time.

The angle was excellent. She could shoot without having to look her husband in the eye. Just as she had hoped. Regardless of the level of her commitment, she knew she was about to cross a line she had never crossed. Lindsey aimed at her husband, took a deep breath, and pulled the trigger.

***

Lindsey stared at the tiny, red light flashing. She punched the code in once again. The red light flashed again. She had no idea why it was not opening. She was certain she had put the right code in. Unless . . .

*The scumbag probably changed it without telling me.*

She looked at her husband's body still lying there bleeding and motionless. She had no hopes for help coming from there. She was vexed because it was a crucial part of her plan. Yet, she knew there was nothing she could do about it and that she had to act fast. She headed outside.

But from the doorway, she saw a dark figure disappear behind the wall at the end of the corridor. She saw the figure but for a second. Then, she heard a noise that sounded like steps, only a few, maybe two, possibly three, but definitely steps. There was someone else here!

Lindsey hadn't prepared for such a thing, and it scared her to death. She had been certain that Sam would be alone tonight. She was aware of her husband's filthy affairs to an extent, and she figured this house was probably where he conducted them, who knows how many times. But it didn't look like that. The figure, being all shadowy, the way it moved and disappeared behind the wall. It didn't seem like a woman just casually sneaking out to the kitchen for evening snacks or something. No. Besides, Lindsey had just listened to Sam talking with someone online, and during that time, not a single soul had been in the house. She'd seen no one and heard no one. So where had the figure been all this time? Maybe—

Maybe Sam really was alone tonight. Maybe that figure had just intruded now, the same way Lindsey had earlier. Maybe she wasn't the only one who had picked tonight to sneak into Samuel Hayes's house?

Whatever her thoughts were about its chances, she didn't dare brush off this idea, and it terrified her. Because she had seen the figure, hadn't she? Or just her nerves were on the verge of collapsing and they had made her eyes play a trick on her? But there was no doubt that her ears had heard the floor creaking right where the figure had disappeared behind the wall. No, it wasn't her nerves. No tricks, no hallucination. It was real. Somebody was here.

She considered her next move. Maybe she had to kill someone else? She had weighed the possible risks and consequences of murdering her husband, and she had figured that having a rock steady alibi would provide her with impunity. But offing a total stranger to make the police investigate a double murder with an unknown suspect? No, it was too much of a risk. Far more of a risk than leaving a witness behind, who wouldn't be able to identify her anyway. But would she be better off if she knew before she left who that shadow belonged to?

A voice interrupted her train of thought.

"Hey!" The voice was shaking, and it was coming from the kitchen.

Lindsey dared not move or speak.

"Listen . . . if you're still there . . . I have no idea who you are, and I don't care . . . But I'm not with Sam. I came shortly after you. And I don't want any trouble, don't want anything. I snuck in here too, so I won't fuckin' go to the police, if that's what you're afraid of. And I didn't see your face, so I can't identify you anyway. I just wanna get out of here. Just as you do, I suppose."

Lindsey couldn't believe her ears.

"You hear me? I think none of us wanted any of this. But it's not too late. You did what you came for—oh God . . . I just wanna go home . . . What do you think? We go our separate ways and forget all of this."

Lindsey had no way of knowing if she could afford to believe the voice, but it sounded honest.

And the guy's words actually matched Lindsey's thoughts. He might be a witness but the mask on her face had surely done its job.

But Lindsey had to make sure she wouldn't undermine the service her mask was doing for her, so she ruled out replying. She must not leave the slightest clue by her words or voice. Lindsey focused on a more pressing question—was he armed? If not, she figured she could either just get out of there or gun him down first, and then leave. But if he did have a gun, he could shoot her on her way out. Although, that didn't seem likely. The things he said they way he talked and the very fact that he had unnecessarily spoken out of the dark suggested that he had no such will. Which would all change, however, if Lindsey decided to go after him. Unknown figure or not, she better not to improvise, Lindsey figured.

It was time for her to disappear and let the other one enjoy trying to figure out what to do with the body. She began moving toward the entrance. But a new thought made her stop. Maybe she could smuggle Sam's own gun out from the room and use that to shoot the guy. And then, just place the guns next to the bodies, as if they had executed each other. All it would take would be to sneak into the large room, remove Sam's gun from his desk drawer, assuming he still stored it in there, and shoot the other guy. But again, if he's got a gun too, the next dead body could very well be hers.

Only a few silent minutes passed while Lindsey considered this, her eyes bouncing back and forth between the door to the large room and the turn in the corridor.

Then, she reminded herself what her thoughts were about improvisation and quickly arrived to the bottom line: this wasn't the right time to take risks beyond necessary. She decided. It is time to wrap this up and get out. The plan she had worked out with Elizabeth must be good enough.

She continued her way out. She was only two steps from the turn in the corridor.

"How much for you to let me go?"

Lindsey gasped and her hand went to her mouth, covering up the scream that wanted to come out.

"Hey! You hear me? How much you want? There's a safe in this room. Whatever's inside, all yours . . . One million. At least."

Horrified, Lindsey retreated to the small bedroom, and using all of her strength, tried to prevent herself from breaking down and crying. *God, he's still alive!!*

She started pacing and panting, and she could hear the conversation between her wounded husband and the terrified-sounding stranger. Every exchange just made her think even more—what now?

Then, an insufferable thought overran her mind. *Oh fuck, did he call the cops?* Lindsey tried to overcome her growing panic and focus on thinking this through. *Did he have his phone on him when I shot him?* Her husband had never been much of a phone person. In fact, he tended to leave it all over the place. But that didn't give an answer to her burning question: *Does he have it now?*

Lindsey's panic lessened as she realized that if Sam knew the cops were minutes away, he never would've even started to talk to the other guy. That would have achieved nothing except risking staying alive until help got there. No, all he'd do is just stay quiet, lie low, and watch. His phone could be broken, dead battery or anything else. Him yelling out and trying to deal with the guy could only mean one thing: Sam was in no position to call for help.

"Alright. So you're trying to tell me that two people who don't know each other and never talked to each other picked the same day, almost the same minute, to break into my house and kill me?"

"I don't wanna kill you!!"

"Yeah, whatever. The point is you came here at the same time. That's what you're saying."

"I know how it must sound, but I swear it's the truth."

"Okay, fine. Lucky you didn't crash into each other coming through the door."

Lindsey breathed a little easier. Clearly, her husband didn't believe the third person existed. And that could work out for her pretty well. As long as those two were busy trying to work each other, they likely would not leave their spot. Until it changed, Lindsey wasn't in the mood for making a move either. It gave her time to go through her options.

She could wait for her husband to faint and likely bleed out. Or even if he was strong enough not to do so, that gun must have been in that drawer today, as it always was, so Sam certainly had taken it. So, one way or another she might end up having only one opponent left to deal with. Then all she'd have to do was swap the unknown's gun with hers and get out, just as it had occurred to her, leaving two dead bodies and two fired guns behind. But the biggest problem in all this still applied; no matter how many guns were in the house, there was definitely more than Lindsey would be comfortable with. Either way, the option of fleeing was not an option until her husband's heart ceased to pound. She had to wait. Wait until this utterly surreal Mexican standoff started to conclude itself, and then she just had to finish it.

"Hey, you! Wherever you are," Lindsey heard Sam shouting. "I'm talkin' to you, dear other stranger who broke into my home today. The thing is, I can't really do business with this one, here. But what about you? Whatever it is you're after, I can assure you, there's enough money in the safe for you to reconsider things. You can leave as a rich man. Way richer than when you got here. And you won't be wanted for murder. Or at least you'll be wanted for one less murder. What do you say?

Lindsey had already considered her husband dead and let him go. But hearing Sam talking again basically to her unknowingly didn't twist her emotionally too much. She was busier hating herself for not having checked Sam's body to ascertain he was dead. Even more for not putting another one in his head to be sure.

\*\*\*

"Listen. There might be another way. I got my laptop on the desk. I can use that to get help. So let's make a deal—you let me go get it, then we gonna be friends. Plus, you'll get the money."

"Do it!"

*Oh, shit, the internet,* Lindsey thought. Quickly but quietly, she stepped out of the room, reached down to the router from the doorway, and carefully switched it off. She moved back inside the room and waited.

"Nice trick, asshole!"

"What?"

"No internet."

"How?"

"Quite a mystery, huh?"

Lindsey felt another modicum of relief. This confirmed that Sam hadn't called anyone earlier, otherwise he wouldn't have bothered with the internet. Besides, somebody would've arrived by now.

\*\*\*

Lindsey's entire body was slowly cramping up from not moving. She took a few soft steps in the small bedroom, but she was wearing a leather jacket, a noisier kind of clothing. Upper body, arms—she had barely moved them at all, even though she didn't really believe her husband could actually hear the noise of calfskin friction through the wall. Still, even that she didn't want to risk. Popping her fingers was out too, although it would have delivered more relief than a cigarette.

As she was trying to figure the situation out, Lindsey realized that Elizabeth still hadn't heard from her. Should she send her a little heads-up? Lindsey contemplated this for a bit but she figured it was too early for warning messages. They had established a few hours time span to get this done so she could still make it. They could still have their movie night together and someone delivering both their pizza and their alibi, just as they had planned. But this scenario required Lindsey to find a way to sort this whole thing out very soon.

During the minutes when Sam and the other guy weren't talking, Lindsey worked on alternative solutions. Although the interior walls were relatively thick, she could hear everything quite clearly between the two men. As much as she could work it out from the voices and noises, she figured her husband was in the corner or somewhere behind the sofa. Even if she could shoot through the wall, she would be shooting blind. Same from the other side, but her husband had already been lucky against Lindsey's gun once today. It would be too dangerous, if not straight out nonsense to start pumping bullets into the wall between them. Especially after having managed to miss him already without the assistance of a wall.

Lindsey waited until the two men started arguing, and then she took a little walk around in the room. She had to move a bit. Then, she spotted something next to the bed—her husband's cell phone was charging. She was right about Sam having no opportunity to call for help. She just hadn't known exactly why. But just as this question met an answer, another question popped up: *Why did Sam tell the guy he left it in the car?*

Lindsey pondered what to do and figured that nothing would be best for now. Her lead ahead of the other two was bigger than she thought.

***

"Alright. You just sit tight over there . . . drink and . . . stay alive. I need some time out there. Just . . . just leave me a little. Okay?"

"Sure, take it easy. Keep your shit together. And I take the advice, all of it."

Lindsey couldn't believe what she had just heard. The two of them had made a deal. More precisely, her husband seemed to have managed to trick the other one. She considered allowing the guy to leave the house if he really was going to get the phone. It crossed her mind to let him out, quietly go after him, and shoot him outside. A silenced shot. Unlikely Sam would hear it. Then, she could wait a little while and show up as the innocent wife who wanted to surprise her husband. There was no way that Sam would be suspicious of her. She could simply step in front of him, and before he realized what was going on, kill him. And it'd be over.

But no! If Sam had lied about his phone to lure the guy out of the house, no doubt it was so Sam could get the phone and call for help. Then why not just wait for Sam to walk into the small bedroom and shoot him. Assuming he would come unsuspicious, which was not guaranteed. Maybe he lied to the guy about the phone, but that didn't mean he didn't believe in the third person at all.

Lindsey heard the man sneaking out and came to the conclusion that the guy's actions outside were less important now. Whether he ran or searched for the phone didn't matter right this second. Her husband was the priority she had to deal with first. Everything else would come later.

But then, another option rocketed into her brain, a possible way to 100% secure herself. The problem, though, was that she would have to take a risk from the unnecessary kind. But if she succeeded, she would be untouchable.

What if she were to let her husband make that call? There was not a doubt in her mind that he would tell the police that an armed man was in his house. So, if she killed Sam after that and left before the police got there, they'd still be looking for a male shooter.

The idea of a male killer-for-hire who had worked for the wife might occur to the police, but since no such thing had happened, there wouldn't be anything to prove. This way, she would lose her place in the group of suspects once and for all. However, the fact that the police would be on their way here held a tremendous risk. But the win could also be tremendous if she succeeded. The hillside was huge, and she knew it relatively well. She could stay under the radar and make her way to the city. She could rush straight to Elizabeth, or Elizabeth could even come and pick her up somewhere. All this plan needed was for Sam to call 911, say a man is trying to kill him, and then no one on earth would ever call the two women to account.

What's more, the concept of "two men killed each other" was still on the table. If she were still to decide to kill the unknown guy with her husband's gun, assuming the guy's still loitering around outside, then she really could make the whole thing look like a double execution type of situation and they might even close the case. But this might shelter too many problems. Once the police swarm the area, who knows how many clues and suspicious details they would uncover that might make them keep at it. No, it was better to avoid the second murder. If Sam says it's a he, and then Lindsey kills him and flees before law enforcement joins the party, from that point on, let them have fun searching for that he.

Lindsey decided. She stepped out to the corridor and quietly started backing up to the door of the bathroom. Her hand was already gripping the handle when she remembered that the door squeaked. In the least, it had been pretty noisy a few days ago. And she had no awareness of Sam having done anything about that. Whatever she was going to do, she knew that she couldn't stay here in the corridor. She was constantly watching the large room's door and holding the bathroom door handle. But she didn't dare open it. If the dry hinges made a sound, everything could go straight down the toilet. She took her hand off the handle and quickly relocated herself to the living room through the arched opening.

Lindsey's entire evening had been one continuous, adrenaline-fueled roller coaster, but the seconds she had just spent in the corridor released so many hormones in her system that only the first words of her "resurrected" husband could match it. Lindsey had to chill down somehow, otherwise she wouldn't be able to pull the trigger when the time came. She took a few deep breaths and felt the buzzing in her limbs slowly running down. Until her husband's words interfered, just like earlier when she was on her way out.

"Hey! Are you still here?"

Lindsey heard Sam calling out, presumably for the other guy. She trembled a little but stood still behind the wall and waited.

"You hear me? You still there?"

Only a few seconds passed before a sharp, double beep from above pierced the silence. *The guy is at the car*, Lindsey thought. At that moment, Lindsey heard what she had been waiting for—her husband getting up on his feet and going to the door.

The chain of events she had hoped for had just begun.

# Chapter 19

"Oh my God!" Sam broke down quietly. Despite the shock he didn't let his guard down and kept watching the doors through the gap under the sofa.

"He lied all along!" Lindsey shouted again from the kitchen. "His phone was in the house! And he just called the police."

"God! You fuckin' bitch! Jesus!" Sam was horrified and getting louder. The growing anger caused by his wife's words offset the pain caused by his wife's bullets.

"But listen to me!" Lindsey continued. "We still have time before the cops get here. You still can get what you came for. If Sam dies, you're free to go and take the money from the safe with you. You have my word!"

"Fuck you, you vicious slut!!"

"I know the combination. I will open the safe for you, and you can take everything," Lindsey relentlessly carried on talking to Austin completely ignoring her husband's insults.

"No, no, don't listen to her!' Sam shouted. "She doesn't know shit! I changed it a few days ago. You only get the money if I live. I'm your only chance. She can't open the safe. And if she can't offer you money, she has to kill you too."

"He's lying! I can open it! And everything in it is yours!"

"No!! Don't believe her!"

Austin listened all this yelling standing in the corridor turn. His head was about to explode. Nevertheless, a few pieces started to fall into place.

*That's why the front door was open*, Austin thought as he tried to put the puzzle together. *She had a key.* That's why he didn't hear a shot when he first got there. Only pacing and like somebody was searching for something. She must have fired minutes earlier when Austin was still outside the house.

And then he recalled an earlier argument he had with Sam.

"Oh yeah, and I'd rather shoot you and rummage through the whole house, instead of just gun-forcing you to give it over, right?"

"Maybe you thought you knew where to look for it, so no need to risk it."

The beeping sound. That's why he saw the figure straightening up behind the desk. The safe must be there, and she tried to open it after shooting Sam. She thought she knew the combination so no need for her husband. But why? Why did she want that money? If her husband was dead and she was above suspicion, it would have landed at her, anyway. Or not?

"Don't listen to him!" Lindsey yelled. "He only says that to have you on his side. He knows that otherwise—"

"He's telling the truth!" Austin interrupted, even grabbing Sam's attention. "You tried to open the safe after you shot him. But you couldn't."

"No, no, I—"

"I heard the beeps when I came in."

Lindsey was silent. Austin's head cleared up even more. He figured out why she hadn't said a word from the beginning. If he had heard a female voice, gotten away, and gone to the police, the group of suspects would've narrowed down significantly. Obviously, once Sam woke up, she couldn't open her mouth.

Hearing Austin's words sparked a bit of hope in Sam.

"Attaboy!" he said, a little upbeat. "Think about your little girl! You still can have what you want. Only one of us wanna murder here."

"You believe him??" Lindsey shouted. "After he fucked you up with the phone and called the police? I heard every word, he lured you out because he didn't trust you."

"I trust now, God damn it!" Sam yelled to both of them.

"More, when you lied and sent me to the roof? What was that for anyway?"

"To call for help! That's what he did!" Lindsey interrupted. "The police are coming. So make up your mind fast. Or you wanna kill me? Guess your daughter will be really happy to find out the cost of her recovery."

"Is that true?" Austin shouted to Sam. "You called the cops?"

Sam hesitated.

"She tells the truth??"

"Yes."

*Oh, God. Jesus.*

The house was silent.

"Sorry man, I just . . . I couldn't know for sure whether you wanted to kill me or not. If I was wrong and I told you where my phone was, it'd be over for me."

"Don't matter, we're all fucked now," Austin said.

"No, it's not too late yet," Sam said. "The cops are slow and they gotta get up the mountain. Besides, they only know about one gunman. No way I could've known about more, 'til you got back. They only need one person. And we still have time."

"You want your little girl to see a cold-blooded murderer every time she's looking at her father?"

"Shut up, you bitch! Shut the fuck up!!"

While the happy couple was shouting at each other, Austin was silent. At this point, he began to realize that the best-case scenario already went bye-bye. Grab the cash and make off in the dark. That was gone.

Unless he took the gunfight upon himself, killed the woman, and the gratefulness-filled Sam allowed him to empty the safe as previously agreed. But then, Sam would have to take responsibility for the murder of his wife and risk the potential hardships of proving rightful self-defense. But if they managed to fix all of this, that could be a way out. Because the woman could not live. Now, she would be the unpleasant witness. No, that couldn't be. But killing her raised the heaviest question of the day.

How could he look his daughter in the eye ever again? Or anyone else for that matter, including himself staring back from the mirror.

No. Not even up for debate. So only one way left—

"You don't have to kill anyone," Sam shouted to Austin, interrupting his thoughts. "Just help me disarm her. I didn't tell them I was alone. I can say I invited you and you came just at the right time and saved my life. I'll testify, nobody will care what she's spluttering. We'll work this out, I swear! Get the money, your hands will stay clean, and you won't have to run."

Austin became unsure again. The artery nearly throbbed out of his neck.

In fact, Sam's proposition wasn't entirely true since he had told 911 that he was alone in the house. Lucky for him, the dispatcher wasn't around to reveal that.

"Don't listen to what he says, he's just using you!" Lindsey said. "If he makes it, he will turn you in too, since you did break into his place, and you can enjoy your jail time, just—"

"Shut up already!!"

The pressure became almost unbearable. The hull began to capitulate. Austin slowly started to back up toward the entrance.

"You think he cares about you or your daughter? Doesn't give a shit, he was sweet talking you only to—"

Austin heard Lindsey cutting off the sentence before she finished it. The hull snapped beyond saving. Austin whirled around and took off running. Slammed the main door open, shattering the glass. Hopped the railing, landed straight on the slope. His ankle strained a little, but he kept running. Didn't look back, just ran downhill. The first responders would be using the road anyway, Austin figured. The front balcony was already behind his back. He was closing in on the woods.

Then three silenced bangs were released into the night. But Austin heard only two of them.

# Chapter 20

Lindsey was standing on the small balcony for only a few seconds. Then she realized she was critically short of time. And options. Only one option was left—the job had to be finished. Sam had to go, no matter how. He couldn't stay alive under any circumstances. She must kill him now and then vanish.

Lindsey went back into the house. In the corridor turn, she pulled close to the wall and looked out at the main corridor. It was the second time today, but she was much more pressed for time now. She started to move closer to the door of the large room, but suddenly, she stopped. Blood on the floor—Sam!

A moment later, an arm swung from the dark bathroom. The bloody hand on its end transformed into a fist and hit Lindsey's right wrist with tremendous power. Her fingers instantly released the gun as she howled in pain. The gun fell to the floor.

Sam grabbed Lindsey's jacket below her neck and, like a raging bear, pinned her to the corridor wall. The gun was in his left hand now, as he'd swapped it over in the bathroom to free his right hand for the attack. Scared-to-death, tear-drenched eyes stared back at him while he shoved the barrel of the Glock underneath her collarbone. Sam didn't say a word. With his right hand, he pulled her ski mask off, unveiling his wife's face. Her anguished, sweat-soaked, terrified, distorted face.

She did not speak either. No begging, no explaining herself.

Sam's whole body was shaking and his bloody forefinger was slipping around the trigger. "Why?" Sam pleaded as hard as he was holding the gun. "Why???" he repeated, now yelling at the top of his lungs.

Lindsey forced herself to say the emptiest, most meaningless word possible.

"Please," she said.

Sam let go of his wife's jacket and punched her in the face so hard that she slipped along the wall, brushing off a picture. Sam reached over, grabbed the jacket behind her neck, and yanked her back. Despite the impact of the fist and the wall, Lindsey somehow managed to stay conscious, and as Sam pulled her from behind, she aggressively fought back. In Sam's eyes, her black dress began fading away in the dim corridor. Flailing arms and black body spun together with the source of a yellowish light, his wife's short, blonde hair.

At one point, Sam sensed he was falling down and then found they had jointly landed on the ground. He saw his wife's head hit the floorboards as she landed, pinned under him. He dropped his gun somewhere near the other one. While his spouse had been ardently defending herself on feet, now her resistance sensibly subsided.

Through the thickening blur, Sam saw the blonde hair floating inches above the floor. Then the blur turned into black and engulfed everything.

# Chapter 21

Edgar parked his car a few feet away from the yellow police tape strung above the road between a tree and a lamp post. He got out of his car and thoroughly eyeballed the scene. As he had made a habit of throughout the years, he just stood by his car and observed. Most of his fellow detectives tended to rush into the secured area, putting out their half-done smokes, not even once disregarding the administrative requirements of entering. Edgar, however, always waited for a bit outside the public barrier to absorb the initial feel and vibe of the scene before accessing the perimeter and becoming a part of it. It hadn't been any different at his very first crime scene right after the academy. The answer to why exactly he did that never really formulated in his head. But this habit was so the opposite of noticeable or out of place that no one ever asked about it, and he never needed to explain.

This was not his only attribute that had built his reputation at the investigation department. One of them was that night calls didn't particularly wear him down. But this questionable strength wasn't acquired via years of experience; it stemmed from his continuous sleep disorders, like insomnia.

As Edgar reached the tape, an officer guarding the area's integrity stepped in front of him.

"Edgar Evigan, Homicide."

The young colleague took a good look at the badge Edgar held up and nodded as an acknowledgement of having found it real.

"Would you?"

Edgar took the pen and signed the entry log.

"Thank you, sir," the officer said appreciatively and politely lifted the tape for him so he could get through with a minimal amount of stooping.

Edgar threw a little smile as an indication of his thoughts about the enthusiastic colleague's work and went toward the house. The road led further up beyond the house to a dark nothingness and was quite narrow. The slope on the left was densely vegetated, and its continuation on the right dropped steeply down to an abyss after a few feet. Hence, the vehicles on the scene were parked in a line: two patrol cars, an ambulance, and the CSI unit's van. Edgar stopped at the second police car and did his scan around again. Two officers were consulting on the bridge to the rooftop. Edgar instantly could see that one of them was in charge and walked over to him.

"Good evening! How's the situation?" Edgar said.

"Evening! Well, it is quite a situation," the officer answered.

"What do you mean?"

"One of the most unique scenes I've ever set foot in."

"How's that?"

"Owner called emergency. Armed man in the house, already got shot, need help immediately. The call was interrupted, operator hears a few gunshots, then silence. We get here, find three persons. One dead, two unconscious."

"Where?"

"Two inside the house, and the third—" The officer pointed to Austin's body, still lying on the slope.

"The owner's condition is critical, lost a huge amount of blood. He was taken straight away. According to the boys, he's probably in a coma."

"Chance to recover?"

"Early to say. The woman got away with a puffy-punched face and some bruises on her body. No major injury."

"Where is she now?"

"There, in the ambulance. She's quite alright, you can talk with her if you want."

"She said anything yet?"

"Just her name, so far. And who she is."

Edgar looked at the officer, who straight away answered the unasked question.

"The owner's wife."

"Right . . . And what's so unique here."

"The guy was alone at home and reported only one gunman."

"So? Maybe he didn't have time to tell. You said the call was interrupted."

"You don't understand. The operator asked specifically, and he clearly stated he was alone."

Edgar pondered this while walking alongside the officer.

"But what's really interesting," the officer said, "is that there's three guns on the scene. And two ski masks."

Edgar now stopped completely. First he looked at the officer, then the ambulance.

"Where did you find the ski masks?"

"One of them's still being worn." The officer gestured toward Austin again. "The other one is in the house on the floor. Right where the husband and wife were found."

"He wasn't conscious, not for one second?"

"No."

"And her?"

"After her husband was taken."

***

"Ma'am. Look at me! Can you see me?"

Lindsey's eyes seemed rather reluctant to appear from behind her eyelids. She didn't see much through the tears and blood, and in the first few seconds, she wasn't really aware of where she was and what was going on. The familiar corridor, the paramedics and police officers working around her, together with the flashing blue and red lights filtering through the broken glass of the main door certainly did their best to fit all the pieces together in Lindsey's head. The paramedic leaning over her was talking constantly.

"You are safe now. Everything's gonna be alright. We just have to take care of your injuries. Nod if you understand."

Lindsey nodded, hesitant.

"Alright. Are you hurt other than your face?"

Lindsey didn't answer.

"Ma'am, do you feel pain somewhere?"

"Uh, no. I mean . . . my head . . . a little."

The officers were securing the perimeter, and the paramedics were doing their work on human life.

"What's your name?"

"Lindsey, Lindsey Vaughn . . . My husband! Where's my husband?"

"What's his name?"

"Samuel Hayes . . . He called the police. It's his house."

"Right."

"Is he still alive?"

"Yes, but he is in critical condition. He lost a lot of blood and—"

"Did he say anything?"

"Hasn't woken up yet. But don't worry, we do everything we can."

"And the other one? He's alive?"

"No. When we got here, he was already dead."

Lindsey started gasping for breath, her head overwhelmed with swirling thoughts.

"Alright . . . and . . ." Despite what she said to the paramedic, every word, every sound she made hurt terribly. "When do you think my husband's gonna wake up?"

"It's difficult to tell."

Lindsey was silent for a moment, thinking.

"I have to . . . I have to go now."

"What? Ma'am, we need to take care of you first and then go to the hospital. Everything's gonna be okay now, don't worry."

"But I need—" Lindsey stopped.

"Need what?" the paramedic asked. "Do you need something? Are you on any medications?"

Lindsey stared ahead, no answer.

"Ma'am—"

"No," Lindsey finally replied.

"You sure?"

"Yes. I'm fine."

"Alright . . . Shall we contact somebody?"

"No . . . No, it's okay"

Lindsey was getting calmer. At least that was the impression she was trying to make.

***

Lindsey was just sitting in the ambulance, letting the paramedic do his job and thinking about her situation, when a voice addressed her from the vehicle's door.

"Good evening, ma'am."

Lindsey looked him up and down. First impression was that he was a bit paunchy, Liam Neeson with a goatee.

"Lieutenant Evigan. I'd like to ask a few questions. You feeling well enough to answer?"

Lindsey thought through what to say.

"Yes . . . Yes," she answered.

"Great."

"Sir, I think, it would be better to let her rest," the paramedic said with sufficient humbleness.

"You're right, son, but it'll be quick. You just keep doing what you're doing, and if the lady feels unfit to continue, she will let me know."

Lindsey felt weird about the lieutenant's brusque manner. Even though his tone of voice was polite enough, the message itself might not be meant for the paramedic.

"Were you in the house when the man intruded?"

Lindsey was thinking.

"No, I mean, I was here, but I was gonna surprise my husband. We were meant to spend the night separately. And when I came here . . . I tried to help, but . . . I . . ."

"It's alright, calm down," Edgar kindly backed off. "Would you prefer to continue some other time?"

"Um . . . yes . . . That would be better."

"Alright. We'll see you in the hospital tomorrow, we'll talk then. You just get some rest. Okay?"

"Okay," Lindsey answered.

Edgar walked off from the vehicle straight toward the house. The lead officer rejoined him.

"Anything about the gunman?"

"No."

Meanwhile a crime-scene specialist was taking another stack of yellow, numbered evidence markers to the house.

"Make sure she's guarded properly."

"You think there's something more than self-defense?"

"I don't know. But I want to speak with the person who communicated with her first, after she woke up."

"Why?"

"Given that the two men are not particularly in a condition to be interrogated, and one of them is unlikely to ever be, she is the only witness right now."

"Right. That's one of the medics from the first ambulance. We will wire the hospital."

"Thank you."

Edgar had no doubt he was facing a very long night.

# Chapter 22

Edgar and his partner were heading to the hospital in the morning rush. Giordano Mattia Lamberti was fifteen years younger than his partner and had been working with Edgar for about a year, during which he had learned more from Edgar than he had all through the rest of his years as a detective. Edgar had already been considered an exceptional investigative talent when he was Giordano's age. Edgar had regularly ended up in disagreements with his more seasoned colleagues over following his own intuitions, intuitions which evidently led to solving many cases and made the old furniture look less shiny. Those who knew how to handle it got along well with Edgar, and the ones who didn't were soon given a new partner. Giordano had heard plenty of stories about Edgar, accompanied by plenty of beer, and always had a hard time understanding the anecdotes about the confrontations. He had looked up to his partner from the very beginning, and he even delivered an intoxicated confession once, in which he admitted that his opinion of Edgar wouldn't be any different if that fifteen years between them was the other way around.

They were traveling with the traffic in silence when a call came in.

"Evigan."

*"Ed, listen, uh . . . I need you to swing by the morgue."*

"We're on the way to the hospital."

*"I know but the coroner found something in the dead guy's jacket and I'm saying you might wanna go and see."*

"We already have a date set with Evidence Control?"

*"No, it's not all ready yet, just this one you need to see."*

"Alright, when we're done talking to the woman, we'll go straight there."

*"Would be better if you go to the morgue first."*

"They also say that?"

*"I say that."*

"Why, what is it they found?"

*"A message."*

Edgar and Giordano looked at each other.

"What message?"

*"They didn't say, but sure, it's important . . . Look, the woman is guarded, ain't going anywhere. Take a look at that message and then go to the hospital."*

"Okay, we're going now."

*"Good. Then come and report to me."*

"Guarded?" Giordano asked after the call ended.

"Discretely," Edgar replied.

The traffic didn't seem to be in the mood to make life any easier. The tempting idea of turning on the lights never failed to nag at Edgar on such occasions. Wouldn't be his first time utilizing this very tool outside the boundaries of his police authority. It had happened only once during his three decades in law enforcement—back when he had received his detective badge and first outfit his car with police lights. He was rushing to his daughter's school dance performance, and thanks to no one but himself, he was running terribly late. Lights flashing, he made it just in time and even managed not to cause an accident. The ability to drive in such a way on the city roads was a crucial part of his job anyway. At least, that's what he had said to himself that once, but never again. He had felt ashamed as a policeman and guilty as a father. It took him more than a year to tell his daughter why he had picked the very last second to show his face. She felt down about it but showed a level of understanding toward her father that could only be compared to that of a loving mother's toward their rogue child. Edgar had spent the following days feeling like he was ready to swallow an entire magazine.

But what had also happened a few years ago was that Edgar had caught a driver who was using cheap, online-ordered flashing lights to cut through traffic. To uninitiated eyes, the strobe lights that were suction-cupped behind the windshield and the LED grille-mounted lights definitely would've seemed legitimate. But Edgar spotted it.

Later on, the driver claimed in a court of law that he needed the flashing lights to make it to the hospital in time when his mother had one of her asthma attacks. As it turned out, it was nothing but true, and Edgar didn't stand in the way then. He only recorded the license and did his research on the vehicle later. Of course, the young man was found guilty of the unauthorized use of warning lights and unsafe road use, but he walked out with only a penalty and a suspended driver's license.

Edgar often mused over these two cases. He had once used tools given to him as a lawman to try to save what he screwed up as a father, while that man had broken the law as a civilian to try to save his mother.

The idea now did a quick in and out in Edgar's head while he and Giordano were inching along in the congestion. But there was no real temptation; no need to rush to a deceased.

"I hate the morgue," Giordano said, only two blocks away from it.

"Who do you think likes it?"

"That's not what I mean, it's just . . ." Giordano gathered his thoughts. "That's the part killing me the most in this job. Glad, I don't have to spend much time there."

"Killing you more than the crime scenes? The victims lying soaked in their own blood?"

"I know, I'm a sicko, but—"

"Didn't say you're a sicko. That might come, but for now, I only asked a question."

"Uh . . . I don't know, but . . . when we find them in their home or anywhere else out there, no matter how gruesome that is, still . . . they're lying dead where they lived. Home or far away, they are where they belong, a living environment. But when they're resting on a shiny steel tray in a cold room, where they didn't spend one minute alive because they came already dead . . . That's just so depressing to me, sometimes I can't even breathe. I know it sounds weird."

"Too often you think you know things, haven't you been told?" Edgar commented jovially.

"I have," Giordano smiled, but he knew his partner fully understood what he had just said.

\*\*\*

The county coroner building cut an impressive figure with its red brick walls, but it was also out of place considering what was behind those walls. If the sign at the front was ignored, no one would expect to encounter corpses inside. A few centuries old, maybe. It would make a better humble church than a body storage facility.

Giordano was greatly relieved when they only had to meet with the head of the Evidence Control Unit rather than laying eyes on corpses this time.

"Good morning, Katherine!"

"Hello, boys! Thank you for coming. We haven't met before, have we?"

"No, ma'am. Giordano Lamberti, pleased to meet you," Giordano responded fast and offered his hand first.

"Katherine Westmacott, my pleasure."

"What's all this drama for? I was never sent here and not allowed to take anything."

"I know and I'm sorry, but we figured this warrants an exception," Katherine handed over a paper towel in a sealed plastic bag. "This was in the inner pocket of his jacket."

Edgar took the bag and started to read together with Giordano.

To the police,

My name is Austin James Rowe. Tonight I came here to take money from Samuel Hayes. My daughter is in a wheelchair and needed money for her rehabilitation. I am dead but if Samuel is still alive, please PLEASE get him to pay for my daughter's treatment!! He is a rich man and ~~crooked~~ Convince him to help my little girl. He can afford and if you ask him I am sure he will listen to you. Please, even if my daughter lost her father don't let her spend a whole life in a wheelchair!!! Please!

And it wasn't me who shot Sam!! There is someone else here. Find that person!

Austin James Rowe
November 2, 2017

126

"What the hell?"

"Not an ordinary note, huh?" Katherine said, responding to Giordano's reaction.

Edgar held the bag in his hand, silent.

"So, you're not taking it now?" Katherine asked.

"No. Together with the rest," Edgar mumbled, staring in front of him.

"Alright. But what are your thoughts?"

"Well, it could definitely simplify the identification," Giordano started, seeing that his partner's mind was focused elsewhere. "Then we need a handwriting analysis to be sure it's his writing. The content we'll examine later."

"Would you mind taking a picture?" Edgar turned to his partner, indicating he was back on deck.

"Sure."

Giordano grabbed his phone, took a photo of the message on the table, and gave the message back to Katherine.

"This isn't the Science Center, detective. Guests are not taking pictures here," Katherine teased Edgar, a cheeky smile on her face.

"I know, but would you let us leave empty-handed?" Edgar returned the sentiment.

# Chapter 23

Edgar phoned the station on the way to the hospital and tasked one of the desk officers to check on the name. Giordano missed a few turns while looking at Austin's message on his cell.

"Should we mention the note to Mrs. Hayes?" Giordano asked.

"Vaughn. Didn't take her husband's name," Edgar replied.

"Ah."

"And no, don't think we should tell her about it. What do you think?"

Edgar had always been keen to quiz his colleagues, even with unnecessary questions, so he could familiarize himself with their way of thinking and logic.

"Agree. But damn, I'm curious what she would say," Giordano said. "Actually, I'm eager to hear her whole story."

Edgar drove in silence.

"You answered like that on purpose, right?" Giordano asked.

"Yeah, normally I figure the words out and purposefully say them through my mouth."

"You know what I mean. You think I asked something stupid. Of course we don't say anything about the message, at least not now, not in the hospital. But you didn't reply like—"

"What? You out of your mind? That's how I was supposed to reply, right?"

"Well . . ."

"I don't always share what I think out loud straight away, okay? I believe it's best to let the other person think things over and develop their own opinion. Or convince me to change my mind."

Giordano smiled.

*** 

Despite having only minor injuries, Lindsey had been given a separate room in the hospital.

"How you feeling?" Edgar asked politely.

"I'm fine, thank you," Lindsey answered. The little, white Band-Aids all over her face were a stark contrast to her tanned skin.

"Great, glad to hear that. I would like to ask a few questions then, if you don't mind."

"No, not at all. Go ahead."

Edgar stepped closer to Lindsey's bed, while Giordano remained motionless three steps away, holding a pen and a small notepad.

"Tell us, what do you remember?" Edgar asked.

"Almost everything, up until I passed out."

"Right. Then let's start from the beginning. When did you arrive at the house?"

"Not sure about the time. But . . . like around eleven, I guess."

"And then what happened?"

"Um . . . I went inside. I was really quiet, because, as I said yesterday, I wanted to surprise my husband. I kind of tiptoed on the stairs too. I was supposed to be busy yesterday, but I managed to get rid of everything and free up my evening. So, I went in and . . . it was way too quiet. Really quiet, like . . . nothing. But his room was bright. I was in the corridor, but I felt like there was something wrong. It was weird. So I pushed the door in and . . . Oh my God . . . I . . . there was . . . I saw . . . blood . . . on the floor. I called his name and . . . and he shouted at me. *'Lindsey, run, get outta here!'* I panicked.

"I wasn't sure where he was, I thought maybe behind the sofa and I was gonna go there, I was gonna run over to him, but it was like I couldn't move and he kept yelling, *'There's somebody here, get outta here. Run!'* I don't know how, but I turned around and went for the front door.

"Then I saw someone coming at me, coming out of the living room. He was pointing a gun at me, like really, I mean really close. But somehow . . . like an instinct, I managed to grab his gun before he could fire. And then we were fighting, the guy was pulling me all over the place, and he hit me, really hard, and dropped his gun. Sam kept yelling my name. At some point, the guy just stopped and ran outside and I . . . I was in shock and . . . I guess, I don't know . . . maybe it was instinct, I picked up his gun and ran after him.

"It hurt really bad where he'd hit me and I felt really dizzy, but I kept going. When I got up to the balcony, I saw him running down the slope, and I shouted at him to stop and—"

"Why?" Giordano interrupted unexpectedly. "I mean, why not let him go? You had his gun, why not go back to your husband straight away?"

"No . . . I was scared, he had a mask on, I didn't want him to go. I mean, what if they never caught him and he came back and tried again? I didn't want, I . . . I didn't want to kill him, I just shot after him, I tried to stop him, I didn't want . . ." Lindsey was becoming more hysterical and teary.

"It's okay, calm down, it's alright. It's fairly understandable. Just relax." Edgar was comforting her, but in the meantime, he threw a look at Giordano to make it clear that Giordano should still remain silent. "What happened after you shot him?"

"I saw him fall, but . . . I couldn't, I didn't see where I hit him. It was dark and my eyes were full of blood. But I saw him moving. And I felt very light-headed and was worried I was going to faint. Then Sam called my name again. I ran back inside and he was bent over, like stumbling in the corridor. Covered . . . and I mean, covered in blood, like . . . I don't know, so I ran up to him but I didn't know what to do. I grabbed him, he hung onto me and . . . then I was gonna call an ambulance, but . . . I don't know. I remember feeling really dizzy and couldn't hold him up anymore and . . . I fell on the floor and he fell with me and . . . that's all. I don't remember anything else."

Edgar inhaled deeply. Giordano kept scribbling.

"So you didn't know your husband already called us?"

"As I just said, that's all I remember. I passed out. I don't know if he called before or after. But he did. And . . . I hope I can tell him that . . ." Lindsey's face was soaked in tears.

Both detectives stood silent, patiently waiting for Lindsey to settle down. Then, Edgar spotted something on the bedside cabinet. Something that didn't necessarily stick out, but Edgar had been around long enough not to let it go unnoticed.

"Ma'am . . . Have you contacted anyone since the incident?" Edgar asked.

Lindsey looked up at Edgar, still wiping her tears.

***

*"What are you doing? Why you calling this—?"*

"Hi, listen . . . um, something terrible happened. Sam was attacked. Somebody came and shot him. He's alive, thank God, but he's in critical condition. Still unconscious, they say. And, uh—"

*"Lindsey, what the—"*

"I'm heading to the hospital now. But don't worry, I'm fine. And the man who shot Sam . . . uh . . . is dead. I just spoke to a police officer. He said it's all gonna be fine. So don't worry. I just don't know how long they'll keep me in the hospital so I might need you to come and get me some of my stuff. I'll let you know when you can visit, and I'll give you my keys. Okay? Anyway, we talk later. Bye."

***

"Yes, I called a friend of mine from the ambulance," Lindsey said. "I told her what happened. I just had to talk to somebody."

"I really like your phone," Edgar said looking at the cell phone on the cabinet.

Giordano found it odd how his partner didn't comment anything on Lindsey's answer and steered the topic of the conversation to the phone instead.

"Uh, yeah, it's just a second phone. I bought it recently."

"I see," Edgar said.

"Sometimes I just enjoy staying away from smart phones, social media and all, you know . . . But still, good to have a phone for emergencies and such."

"Sorry, I, myself, am a huge fan of all these modern smart things so I don't get what you're saying at all."

Edgar delivered his line in such a sarcasm-soaked manner that it made both Lindsey and Giordano smile, thus lifting the mood significantly.

"Um, would you name the friend you called?" Edgar asked. "Just for the record."

"Of course. Elizabeth. Elizabeth Rantzen, an old friend from high school."

Giordano recorded the contact details Lindsey provided.

"Well, thank you, ma'am," Edgar said. "Your official statement will be recorded later. But you've already helped a lot."

Giordano looked at his partner mildly surprised, and Edgar nodded toward the door, indicating they were done here, time to go. The two detectives said goodbye and left the room.

"Where were you going with the phone?" Giordano asked once they were in the corridor.

"Let's talk in the car."

"Right."

They walked in silence all the way down to the parking lot.

"So, the phone," Giordano said after his seatbelt tongue clicked into the buckle.

"What did it look like to you?"

"You think it's a burner?"

"Unless we buy that "staying away from smart phones" thing."

"Yeah, I admit, that wasn't the strongest part of her story."

"It wasn't, right? Speaking of which, what do you think about it?"

"Her story?"

"Yep."

"Overall, sounds credible to me."

Edgar didn't response.

"You disagree?"

"No-no, I agree."

"But?"

"But, all these weird circumstances . . . like, too many guns and masks on the scene, that mysterious "someone else" in that letter. And the fact that they found a "someone else" right there on the spot . . . It all could make a slightly different story, no?"

"Yeah. And if she is the "someone else" she might have gotten some help. Namely from this Elizabeth. That's what you're saying, right?"

Edgar nodded, eyes on the road.

"We could have asked her to hand the phone over," Giordano said. "I know she could refuse, but . . ."

"Yes, we could have. But why didn't she get rid of it? Send it down the toilet or something. Why did she leave it in front of us like that? She knew we were coming."

"Did she?"

"After what happened of course she'd expected a visit from the police. Plus, I actually told her last night that we'd talk today."

"Ah, alright."

"So why was the phone right there? And why did she choose to make a phone call from the ambulance?"

"Part of the blameless wife act."

"Yep. And the phone on the cabinet, staring at us? Could be a bluff or—" Edgar stopped here and glanced at his partner.

"There was nothing on it to hide," Giordano said.

"Exactly. The "blameless wife", as you said. Whether it's an act or real, I don't think we would've gotten much further by snatching that phone."

"Alright, so first, let's find out if she's guilty or not. And if she is, then we can get back to whether she got help or not."

"Right on."

"By the way . . ."

"Yes?"

"Why didn't we ask a bit more? You know, push a few more questions to see if she'd contradict herself."

"Because, for now, her answers are better than our questions."

"I see. And how can we improve our questions?"

"First, we check on this friend of hers. Then we talk to the paramedics who were around when she woke up. To know what she said to them and hopefully somebody heard what she said on the phone."

"Okay . . . sure."

"And also I want to check the call Hayes made and hear what exactly he said to the operator."

Giordano didn't comment on these ideas any further nor ask about why. He knew there was no need. Edgar was not the kind of detective who deliberately cut the less experienced partner out of his thoughts just to look smarter. And Giordano figured he could do some contemplation regarding Edgar's reasons before hearing his explanation. Only a few blocks of driving down the road and Edgar's ideas already seemed to make a sufficient amount of sense.

# Chapter 24

"What, you're staying here?" Giordano asked as he stared at Edgar still sitting in the car, the engine killed, the parking brake on.

"No, it's just..." Edgar started. "This is the part I hate."

"Who do you think likes it?"

Edgar gave his partner the side-eye while Giordano tried his best to display a confident look to match the brazen words he'd just spoken. Tried, at least. Despite the relative short time they had spent working together, the two detectives had gained a deep knowledge of one another. Therefore, many of their exchanges concluded with looks that served as perfect replacements for words. They got out of the car almost simultaneously.

They had received the address yesterday, but they had decided to wait one day before doing the visit. It hadn't been too hard to find the family given there was only one Austin James Rowe in the county records. Austin's girlfriend, Jessica, had already confirmed his identity, but she hadn't yet been put through questioning.

"I know you, and I know how much this isn't to your liking," Giordano said, initiating a conversation again while pacing on the walkway that led to the porch. "But now you seem even more anxious than usual. Don't freak me out!"

His effort did not meet success of any kind. Edgar remained silent and resigned all the way up to the front door. Besides his numerous, well-known attributes and habits,

Edgar had a few lesser known ones too. Observing the crime scenes from the outside before entering didn't particularly influence his work. But the trouble he tended to have in situations like the one he was about to encounter certainly did. Whether victim or perpetrator, contacting the relatives in person always challenged the hell out of his mental well-being. Austin Rowe's family was the worst possible scenario since they fit into both categories.

The house was a modest, one-story family home with a homemade wheelchair ramp leading up to the front door. A car in the driveway indicated that they were probably home. Giordano pulled open the screen door and knocked, then he and Edgar waited on the small front porch for the inevitable. A woman in her thirties came to the door, and both detectives registered how attractive she was, despite her grungy sweatpants, matted hair, and smeared makeup. Edgar identified himself and his partner and verified that the woman was Austin's girlfriend, Jessica. She welcomed the two detectives in just as politely as she would any other guests, but she couldn't mask her emotional state.

The atmosphere inside was no different than what could be expected under the circumstances. The interior looked homey, yet it felt empty and lifeless. It was silent; no music or TV on, nor any other noises of life.

"Can I get you something?' Jessica said as she led them into the living room. "Soda? Or I can make some coffee if you like."

"No. I mean, yes, sure. Hell, it must be a whole lot better than what we drink at the station,' Edgar said awkwardly, attempting to joke and ease the tension.

"Thank you," Giordano added.

As Jessica went into the kitchen, the two officers noticed Austin's daughter at the other end of the living room. She was sitting by the window in a wheelchair looking out at the backyard. A black cat on her lap seemed to have just woken up from a deep dream. Edgar and Giordano greeted Austin's daughter, and she deftly turned around and rolled up to them using the metal hand rims. The cat appeared less than thrilled to see the strangers but didn't jump out of her lap.

The detectives were astonished at how beautiful she was. Her face was not that of a model, screaming for magazine covers, but at sixteen, she was a natural beauty with the kind of charm that inevitably captures the eye. And she hadn't even said a single word.

"Hello. I'm Cynthia." She greeted them warmly, but her eyes were red and swollen. "Please make yourself comfortable."

"Thank you."

There was no way on earth to tell which of the detectives was more nervous. After introducing themselves to Cynthia, they sat down on the sofa, and she rolled herself back to the window, making sure not to turn her back to the officers.

She then just sat there in silence looking out the window and cuddling the cat. Edgar and Giordano were feeling terribly uneasy. Both would have loved to say a word to her, to start up a conversation about anything at all while Jessica was making their coffee, but neither could—or dared—come up with a topic. Finally, Edgar went ahead and broke the silence, although only with a kind of half measure.

"You got pen and paper?" he asked his partner.

"Uh . . . yep, I got it."

After sitting through a few more silent seconds, Giordano forced himself to give it a try.

"What's your cat's name, Cynthia?" he said.

"Charlie."

"Ah, so it's a boy," he said.

Cynthia looked up from her lap. "No," she said.

Giordano cringed, convinced he had just embarrassed himself. Edgar, however, was encouraged.

"Sure," Edgar said. "My middle name, for example, is Blaine. Also unisex." Edgar leaned slightly forward toward Cynthia. "And allegedly he is a detective too."

The tiny smile appearing in the corner of Cynthia's mouth felt like a monstrous achievement to Edgar. Also Giordano appreciated his partner's teasing more than he ever had.

Just then, Jessica returned with a plastic tray that held two cups of steaming coffee, a porcelain jug full of milk, and a third cup filled with sugar cubes.

"Don't know how you like it, so I got everything."

"That's really kind of you, ma'am."

"Thank you, ma'am."

Besides words, they both thanked her for the kindness with a gesture. They usually drank their coffee black, but this time around, neither the milk nor the sugar was left untouched. Jessica sat herself facing the officers and didn't hesitate to ask her question.

"So, are you going to tell us what happened exactly?" she asked. "Because I was called in for identification, but they didn't really tell me anything. Only that . . ." She turned and looked at Cynthia, who was looking down at the cat while she petted her, then Jessica looked back to the officers. "They said Austin broke in somewhere and out of self-defense"—she leaned forward and lowered her voice, as if it would prevent Cynthia from hearing her—" they shot him."

Now all three of them turned and looked at the girl, who was now staring at the world beyond the window and stroking the snoozing, curled up Charlie.

"Um, maybe if we could speak in private," Edgar suggested.

"Don't bother," Cynthia said without looking at them. "You can talk here."

Neither Jessica nor the detectives forced this idea further, so they all remained seated and continued.

"Right . . . well, still a lot of questions around," Edgar said, "and we don't want to jump to conclusions here. Which is why we'd like to ask a few questions first. That could be a great help for us."

Jessica nodded.

"So first," Edgar said, "how long you been with Austin?"

"A little more than three years."

"And how long have you been living together?"

"I moved in . . . a year and a half ago. Right?" She turned to Cynthia, as a courtesy of trying to involve the girl in the conversation.

Cynthia nodded, still staring outside.

"So, you are unmarried, is that correct?" Edgar said.

"Yes. We were going to get married this summer but—" Jessica glanced at Cynthia. She could only hope the girl didn't hear or understand what she was going to say. But she couldn't tell.

"When did you last see him?" Edgar asked quickly.

"The night before. He left very early for work."

"What did he do for a living?"

"He was a production operator at Slyndell Automotive."

"Right." Edgar paused for a few seconds thinking about the next question. "So, the night before, did he say or do anything . . . strange or unusual?"

"No. He just . . . he just said he was gonna come home very late." Jessica lowered her head. "But that wasn't unusual."

"Alright," Edgar said. "How about lately?"

"What do you mean?"

"Did he behave strangely or say something, anything that might have given you the idea that he was up to something? Like . . . he appeared to be more nervous than usual or . . . went to a place more often than he used to or came home later than he was supposed to. Anything like that."

"No," Jessica answered in a whisper. She sounded unsure.

"Did you see him with someone who . . . I don't know, looked or behaved suspicious?" Edgar asked. "Someone you'd never seen before?"

"No."

"No weird phone calls, nothing?" Giordano extended Edgar's question.

"No. Can't recall anything like that."

"That's alright," Edgar said.

"About the other thing . . ." Jessica started reluctantly.

"Yes?"

"I mean, yes . . . recently, he seemed like, more anxious than before . . . He ate much less, he talked less and . . . many times, we felt like, he was somewhere else in mind completely.

The detectives patiently listened to the woman as they sipped their coffee, neither realizing that Giordano had totally forgotten to put the aforementioned pen and paper to use.

"But how's that supposed to be strange? Given the circumstances, we—" Jessica stopped mid-sentence again, but Edgar gave her time to pick up and continue. "Look, I'm sure you know this period has been very hard for all of us. We left no stone unturned, we tried as hard as we possibly could to try to get the money we needed, but nothing. No success. It took him really hard. We used to argue a lot. But . . . lately, he never raised his voice, not one loud word in the house"—Jessica was tearing up—"probably because he already decided . . . but didn't tell anyone."

Edgar looked at the girl again, defeating his intention of quickly responding to Jessica's words. Edgar could see that Cynthia's eyes were dry, but her expression was hard to read, as she was still staring at the backyard, her face at a right angle to Edgar. Edgar was engrossed in studying the girl for so long that Giordano had to jump in.

"Ma'am, you couldn't have known what he was up to,' Giordano said. "The man whose house he broke into is still in a coma. But he can wake up anytime, and then, hopefully, he's going to tell us with his own words what happened. For now, we can't say for certain if Austin had any intention of harming someone."

"What do you mean? Then why did he have to die?" Jessica asked, getting even more emotional.

"Uh, look ma'am"—Giordano groped for an answer—"he went inside that house. That's breaking and entering. And he was armed, so . . ." Giordano cut this sentence. "But we don't know yet if he assaulted anyone. There is still evidence to analyze."

"But then . . . what . . ."

"I'm sorry, we can't tell you more about an ongoing investigation," Giordano said. "The most important thing now is for you to be strong," he continued trying to calm Jessica. "And don't believe anything you hear about Austin, except what you hear from us. As soon as we have something new, we will contact you."

The two detectives didn't want to push their questions for too long. They didn't direct any questions toward

Cynthia, and none were asked by her. They hadn't gotten too far with Jessica, but they turned to trying to put some hope into the grieving family. They knew that the time would likely come to put them through further questioning, but until then, Edgar did not want Jessica and Cynthia to be harassed.

Cynthia stayed by the window after she said goodbye to the detectives. Jessica led the two officers outside to the front porch.

"I'm glad to see Cynthia holding up so well," Edgar said quietly.

"Holding up so well?" Jessica repeated, a hint of anger in her voice.

"I mean . . ." Edgar turned his face to the living room for a second but failed to continue the sentence.

"You mean, she didn't cry her eyes out in front of you, or hysterically ask questions about her father's death? I wish she had!"

"But . . ."

"Okay, yesterday she broke down completely and cried, just like me. But today, it's like . . . she's sad, but she . . . seems so calm. I've never seen her like this before. It feels . . . it feels like she already . . . decided that—" Jessica suddenly put her hand over her mouth. She could not continue.

***

The atmosphere in the car wasn't much of an improvement over that in the house.

"You think she was gonna say that . . ." Giordano asked.

"Damn right she was," Edgar replied.

"Oh, man."

"You know what's the worst aspect of the emotional trauma?

"No."

"Your mind knows that whatever this is, pain and the hollow feeling will last damn long. And if the agony becomes unbearable, the mind tends to seek shelter in a thought."

"What thought?"

"That all of this will last only until you end it. And you find peace and solace once you decided."

"You can't take things for granted based on what she said."

"Based on what we saw."

"We all process these things differently. Just because your cry is the loudest at the funeral, doesn't mean your pain is the gravest."

They both turned silent. Giordano spoke the next words after some time.

"But we're arguing again over something we actually agree on."

Edgar showed no reaction to this statement.

"Did you think about also her situation?" Giordano asked. "Jessica, I mean."

"Yeah, of course," Edgar answered, waiting for his partner to continue.

"I mean . . . I have no doubt she loves that girl. Maybe like her own.

"What are you saying?"

Giordano sighed.

"Just imagine you find someone who's got a daughter. You are with him for a few years, you were gonna get married, then shit happens, the man dies, and you end up alone with a wheelchaired teenage girl who isn't even yours."

Edgar didn't comment. He had to process the fact that he hadn't even thought this through himself.

"Think about that," Giordano continued. "If you were her, what would you do?"

# Chapter 25

"You sure they recalled everything precisely?" Giordano raised the question while he and Edgar were rolling out of the hospital's main gate.

"They're smart guys, I got no reason to doubt it," Edgar answered.

After having paid a prearranged visit to Elizabeth at her workplace, the detectives had checked Sam's 911 call at the communications center. The next step in their course of action was to go to the hospital and talk to the paramedic who first spoke with Lindsey at the scene and also to the one who was with her in the ambulance when she made the phone call.

"But what did you make of what they said?" Edgar asked.

"Well . . ."

"Come on."

"You wake up there that way—bleeding, injured—and your first question is "Where's my husband?" Makes sense. The next one: "Is he alive?" Still fine. And the third? "Did he say something?" Pfft . . . I mean, if I could pick ten questions in a situation like this, none of them would be "Did he say something.""

Edgar smiled approvingly, then nodded slightly at his partner, who saw nothing of all this, as he was so consumed by his heavy thoughts.

"There's something else bothering me," Edgar said.

"Something with her phone call?"

"No. Based on what the paramedic said, nothing suspicious."

"What then?"

"Why was the ski mask on the floor? Okay, assuming it was also Rowe's, it fell out of his pocket on the run or whatever. But if it was hers, why wasn't it on her head?"

"Who knows? Maybe it fell off in the fight."

"That's just it. The lab didn't find any hair on the inside."

"Hair, no, but you read it too. Ski mask was pretty damp, even at the time the sample was collected. Which indicates it was worn."

"That's true. But still doesn't add up. She's wearing it, who knows how long, and someone pulls it off during a fight, cuz it does not just fall off like that—and not one piece of hair stays inside?"

"I think it's plausible. Damn lucky she isn't suffering from hair loss. Or. . ."

"Or what?"

"Or she truly isn't lying . . ." Giordano said, following a brief hesitation. "But . . . no, too many things don't fit here, really. I honestly don't know . . . The problem is that without real clues, evidence, these are nothing more than suspicious circumstances. Even the ski hat without hair can be shrugged off as Rowe's spared one. Or he could even wear both. That's it."

"Sure, he had an extra pair of socks too."

"That, maybe not. But all it takes is her lawyer coming up with something like . . . I don't know, one of them must have been uncomfortable, poorly cut holes or whatever. Even if it sounds a bit far-fetched, as long as you can't prove otherwise, it'll stand in court."

Edgar went quiet again.

"But that's not what bothers me the most." Giordano began to speak again. "If Rowe was really going for the money in the safe, then why didn't he just have Hayes open it for him? Before shooting him."

"He maybe planned it that way, but things went off the rails. Hayes took his own gun, and they wound up in a shootout. That's why they both took cover somewhere."

"Maybe . . . Damn, Hayes really could do us the courtesy of waking up. That would be a hell of a help."

"Sure, it would. But we might wanna do the courtesy of showing some results without his help. What if he never wakes up? Or he doesn't remember anything? Hmm?"

Both of them quietly stared into the traffic ahead.

"Biggest question here, if Hayes spoke about an armed man, how could the wife be guilty?" Giordano had asked the million-dollar question.

"That's a good question."

"And how the hell did even this . . . stationary warfare form between the two of them?"

"What do you mean?"

"Okay, he missed at first, and then kinda figured that Hayes armed himself too, so he didn't dare risk it. Or better, Hayes fought back somehow, took his own gun, and instantly opened fire at Rowe. So no wonder, he went into hiding."

"And what's the question?" Edgar asked.

"Why didn't he just leave all that shit?" Giordano gave the very answer that Edgar had expected. "He got scared because he didn't really anticipate bullets flying toward him, fine. Then why was he wasting so much time in the house? Why not just get the hell out of there in the beginning?"

"Because he still would've been wanted for attempted robbery and attempted murder. And being on the run with no money isn't so much fun."

"Won't argue about that. But then, what was he doing all that time? Can't even stop Hayes from calling 911, and only attacking him again during the call, like a last resort? Nah, come on!"

Edgar just listened and watched the road.

"By the way, you're doing it again," Giordano said.

"Doing what?"

"Coming up with this bullshit explanation while you're actually sharing the very same opinion as me."

"And what would that be?"

"Maybe Rowe had no intention of staying there, at all. But that "someone else" . . . He didn't just make that up."

"Looks like, he didn't."

"Though, I still don't quite understand how it could have been her," Giordano said.

"The more I think of it . . . the mask could be the answer. Simple."

"You mean he didn't see."

"Yeah. You see a figure in the dark wearing a mask shooting at you. What do you say when you call 911?"

Giordano gave it a few seconds of contemplation before he answered.

"Just report an armed man or gunman," Giordano said, "without thinking whether it's Nikita or Léon hiding under the mask."

"Exactly."

# Chapter 26

The lab had finished their work on all the samples collected from the scene, and Lindsey's official statement had been recorded, so the time had come for Edgar and Giordano to pay a visit to the major.

"Alright, what have you got for me?"

"You gonna be impressed, boss," Edgar started.

"I'm so intrigued now."

"Not talking about us, the lab was quicker than usual." Edgar allowed his mouth to present a tiny corner smile.

"Appreciate your modesty, Evigan, but I can't stand you smiling like this, so cut to the chase, if you would."

"But it means nothing but good, boss."

Major Gene Travis Rafferty had been in charge at this police station for about twelve years. He was getting pretty close to his sixties, and his hair was choosing to abandon his skull, rather than decently turning into silver. And the major smiling was a similar phenomenon to Bigfoot or Nessie—there were rumors about it, some insisted they had seen it, but no one ever managed to present proof. And today didn't seem to be a breakthrough on this subject.

"Alright," Edgar said, cutting the lighthearted prologue short. "A simple game: find the matching pairs. So, you got three people and three guns. Two men have taken a bullet, two guns were fired. You want me to draw a sketch?"

"Very funny, Evigan. When this case is closed, remind me to demote you."

Edgar apologized with honesty that was perfectly matched with the degree of how insulted his boss felt.

"The question being—which gun belongs to who and what were they used for? First, there's the Glock. According to the records, it's legally owned by Hayes, totally fine, only his fingerprints were found on it."

"Continue!"

"And the Ruger and the Herstal. Both untraceable. Seems like, at least. No serial number, no prints on them. The latter one lines up with the fact that both she and Rowe wore gloves."

"She explained the gloves with the cold," Giordano interrupted with a smile.

"Stop talking," Edgar said, admonishing his partner.

"Sorry."

"But good point to bring up, we'll get back to that."

The major puckered his forehead.

"Point is, the Ruger is the only clean one out of all three. The Glock and the Herstal were fired. And only the woman made it bullet free. Now, the bullets found in the two guys, all from the Herstal. Five in total—Hayes two, Rowe three. Another three planted all over the walls, two coming from the Glock. So, the other two guns could belong to Rowe, in theory. Although, you might wanna ask who the hell brings two guns to kill one man.

"With one silencer," Giordano added.

"Ah, yes, I forgot. There was a hybrid silencer attached to the Herstal. One could argue it might be odd—two guns, one silencer. But both of them are 9mm, the silencer happened to fit both so, interesting but nothing more . . . Anyway, let's say we accept what she says, which is she took the Herstal from Rowe during a fight and used it to shoot him."

"While he was already running down the slope," Giordano added.

"Yep," Edgar nodded. "She wore gloves, so no prints on the gun. But unlucky for her, in this case, it's not the fingertips that are revealing, it's the hands. Since things are not there where they are supposed to be. Or at least contradict her statement."

"How's that?" the major asked.

"Rowe's gloves had no blood, no gunpowder on them. However, the way her face looked then, whatever did that, should have been bloodied in the process."

"That's pretty thin," the major said. "She can just say Rowe smashed her head into the doorframe or somewhere. If she didn't say it yet, gonna explain it with the head trauma. She didn't remember, that simple. Not gonna be found guilty because of not bleeding all over the place."

"Unfortunately, that's true," Edgar agreed.

"I assume Hayes was not examined for foreign blood."

"He was covered in blood when they found him, but too bad for him, he wasn't treated as a dead body, so the potential clues are all gone," Edgar replied, spicing it up with a pinch of irony.

The major mildly shook his head.

"Also her gloves, though it's just a minor detail," Edgar continued. "So, she was wearing gloves. Nothing special, it was a bit cold that night, for sure. But her body was sweltering when they found her. Which makes one wonder where she sweat that much. Probably in the house."

"So? Wouldn't you get sweaty in a fight that involves fists and guns?"

"I suppose, I would," Edgar answered. "But based on how the paramedics found her, they concluded that she likely spent a certain amount of time in the heated house wearing a jacket and gloves. More than what she said in her statement. Interesting, no? Why didn't she at least take off her gloves? But again, it's just a small thing, worth mentioning, but luckily, it isn't the leader of the weird circumstances."

The major kept the grumpy face, though his nod was slightly more satisfied.

"Also, there are Hayes's wounds."

"What about them?"

"Fortunately, the hospital is staffed with eagle-eyed doctors."

"Elaborate, please."

"When they removed the bullets from his body, they could see that the blood around the two wounds was clotted unequally."

"What?"

"Not to mention the fabricated tourniquet that somebody made from a sock and a belt. We're sure that a significant amount of time passed between the two shots. Of course, without proper lab check, not much we can do with this, but . . . they're saying, because of the blood around the holes, could be even a one or two-hour difference.

"Did you ask her about this?" the major asked. "To see what she'd say."

"Yes, we did," Edgar answered.

"And?"

"She said, of course, she got no idea about what happened there before she arrived. About the time between shots, she said, maybe Rowe missed at first, which led to this standoff, and when she showed up, Rowe tried again. And missed again."

"Steep," the major said. "But possible."

"Yeah," Edgar said. "And if we can't prove that she was there before she said she was, we can't charge her for not knowing exactly why such a long time had passed between the shots."

*\*\**

"Forget about Hayes," Edgar said to his partner after they left the major's office and were back behind their desks. "Let's think of him as dead, and we have to solve this like that. Clues are there, we just have to figure them out."

"Hate to repeat myself, Ed, but—gloves, masks, guns, gunpowder, blood—can't see any of them serving as absolute proof. Gunpowder on her glove? Sure, she fired, can amount to rightful self-defense. Rowe's glove's clean? He could've wiped it off. Hayes's blood is on his wife's jacket? Good luck finding out whether they fought or helped each other. And so on."

"There's always a way to recreate and unravel the events. Always enough clues left, just need to find them."

"I agree, Ed, but this is different. We can solve burglary and murder individually. But if the two blend together, with clues and everything, and after you have like one and a half survivors left . . . then it's pretty damn hard to tell who did what and why. And apparently, this is exactly what we're dealing with right now."

# Chapter 27

Edgar concluded the third consecutive hour of leaning over the crime scene photos, yet he wasn't even halfway done with his second beer. The photos blanketed the better part of Giordano's desk. Basically, nothing but the phones and the computer monitors were visible anymore. Giordano was long gone, so his opinion was never asked.

The photos were separated into groups based on which part of the crime scene the photo depicted. But there was one particular image that distinguished itself from the rest and was given the privilege of having Edgar's undivided attention longer than any other. It was the photo of Austin's message that Edgar couldn't move on from. He kept reading it over and over, despite not even knowing what he was looking for. Oddly enough, this was the first reading material capable of engaging him on this level since he read *Fight Club* twenty some years ago.

The police years that lined up behind him had rolled quite a few things in his way, almost ending his tenure before it was time. Two times, he had wound up thanking only his stellar reputation and his benefactors in the right places for not having to quit law enforcement due to his alcohol problems. Although many more times than twice he considered the possibility of early retirement, solely induced by the failure to solve a case. *Part of the job. No player had ever retired because of a miss. Paperwork is gonna be a bitch*, he kept being told by those few whom he decided to clue in from time to time. Every single one of those points was pretty hard to argue, however, Edgar could never take a break from the feeling of having the brain for this job rather than the stomach.

He was in the middle of looking through the group of photos of Sam's workroom when his eyes suddenly stopped moving. The photo so grabbed his attention that he inadvertently put down his beer bottle on the edge of a small notepad so that it was standing at a steep angle, on the brink of falling over. Edgar took the photo in hand and stared at it for many seconds, then he grabbed a pen and a blank piece of paper. In the process, he toppled the askew bottle, which obediently fell on his lap, spilling its contents on the way and leaving a sizeable stain on his pants above the knee.

Following a healthy amount of swearing, Edgar focused on the picture again, studied it, then started to write something on the paper. Again, he stared at the photo and, in turn, wrote on the paper. Few minutes later, he put the photo aside and only analyzed what he'd written on the paper. And then, all of a sudden, everything fell into place. He sat motionless while the gears turned in his mind. Then, he reached for his cell phone.

*"Ed?"*

"Get yourself together, we got a job to do!"

*"What job?"*

"I'll come and pick you up in half an hour."

*"Where do we go?"*

When the call ended, Edgar slipped the piece of paper and the corresponding photos into a large, yellow envelope. He put on his coat and went for the door, leaving the mess behind, including the beer spillage. But he stopped before the corridor. After a brief contemplation, he took out the paper from the yellow envelope, placed it on the secretary's desk, took a pen from her drawer, and wrote something on the back of the paper. Then, he put it back into the yellow envelope and strode out of the room.

# Chapter 28

Giordano pretty much crash landed in the passenger seat, and Edgar floored it.

"Alright, Ed, what's going on?"

"Yellow envelope."

Giordano grabbed the envelope that was sliding on the dashboard and removed its contents. The additional info from Edgar amounted to no more than the absolute minimum, yet his young partner had it all figured out before they cut through the next intersection. His reaction, though, surpassed Edgar's highest expectations.

"You've been drinking over there?"

"Wow, that is one damn sophisticated nose you got there."

"Also see the stain on your pants. I mean, I don't mind, man, I don't care, but if she smells it too, then—"

"It's non-alcoholic."

"Oh."

"Still on my desk, we can go back. Or fetch a breathalyzer, happy to blow some breath sample for you."

"Okay, okay, fine, I believe you, forget it."

After this point, the two detectives spent the entirety of their trip orchestrating their upcoming visit, discussing it down to the finest details in order to eliminate any chance for misunderstanding or confusion once they got there.

Lindsey was rather surprised hearing Edgar's voice on the intercom. When greeting them, however, she appeared to be quite calm and friendly from the get-go, despite opening the door with messy hair, no makeup, and wearing a robe, which is not what women tend to dream about.

"Wow, some view you got up here," Edgar said when he saw the window looking out at downtown from the living room.

"Yeah . . . We both have a thing for heights and beautiful views," Lindsey added. "Uh, can I get you something?"

"No, thank you, won't be here too long. And again, apologize for the late hour, ma'am, but . . . we thought important news should not wait one minute."

"Well, if it's important, you thought just right. Please, take a seat, make yourself comfortable."

Lindsey sat down on a purple velvet sofa while Edgar lowered himself onto one of the armchairs facing Lindsey. Giordano remained standing two steps away from Lindsey's sofa.

"So . . . any change in my husband's condition, maybe?"

"No. That news, you'd get straight from the hospital via phone call."

"True." Lindsey smiled a smile filled with sadness while picking the bandage under her right eye. "Then, why have you come?"

"We found this message in the man's pocket."

Edgar took a photo out of the envelope and handed it over to Lindsey.

"Don't understand. How . . ."

"Whether it's true or not, what's in it, this is one hell of a try, for sure. A part of it has already been confirmed to be true. After identifying him, we could also ascertain about his wheelchaired daughter. But regardless, he might have tried to murder your husband, but—"

"Might have tried?" Lindsey said, aghast. "He put two bullets in my husband, who's still lying unconscious. What do you mean by *might have tried*?"

"I mean, until we know exactly what went down between the two of them before you arrived, all we can do is assume," Edgar said. "Clues indicating that the man trespassed, fired on your husband, who showed resistance, and . . . that could be why he wrote this message. Like even if he dies, though, there's still a hope, it wouldn't be all for nothing. Probably."

Lindsey gently nodded.

"That last sentence, though, where he implies a third person . . . that does complicate things."

"Trying to draw away suspicion from himself, what's so complicated about that?"

"You might be right. But as for me, what really got me thinking is not what he wrote, but the very fact that he left a message. Trying to achieve his goal, even if he doesn't make it. Desperate attempt, indeed, but given this very specific situation, rather understandable."

"Where are you going with this, detective?"

"There were two of them in that house facing death . . . What if not just one of them left a message?"

Lindsey gulped in a far from subtle way.

"If we assume that a certain amount of time passed between the bullets hitting your husband and your arrival to the scene, and in fact, everything seems to confirm that, then why wouldn't it be possible that your gravely injured husband tried to leave some kind of message too? In case he didn't survive."

"Maybe . . . But . . . What could he want to message about? Farewell to the loved ones, or . . ."

"Could be. But besides that, what other purpose can one think about as a . . . I'm sorry, but as a dying man?"

"Just say what you think, detective. I'm not in the mood for guessing."

"Apologize . . . For me, he might've pretty much tried to expose the shooter."

"You mean . . . he knew that man?"

"Knew or not, he might've tried to expose the shooter."

Edgar took the other photo and handed it over to Lindsey.

"It was taken in the house. Your husband's laptop, lying behind the sofa."

Lindsey was looking at it without any particular reaction, so Edgar continued.

"I agree, can't see much in this picture. But we also made a video recording at the scene. It's much easier to catch what's important in that."

"Is it? And what would that be?"

"You see the blood prints on the keyboard?"

"Yes, I see . . . So? Sam was bleeding heavily, no wonder he covered even the laptop with his blood."

"Absolutely," Edgar agreed. "But if you look closely, you can see, he didn't just cover it. Those are not blood drops or smear marks, rather they look like . . . fingertips, individually on certain keys."

Lindsey looked at Edgar quite a long time then turned back to the photo. This time, she leaned even closer to it.

"I don't know," she said. The keys are black, can't really tell . . . which ones are clean, which ones are bloody."

"Yep, you're right. Still, you can kinda see. I also watched the video and"—Edgar took the sheet of paper out of the envelope and held it up in front of Lindsey—"I wrote down the letters of the keys that are bloody."

WEETYIOSFHMM

"Both E and M clearly have two separate marks on them," Edgar added. "Maybe . . . Anything you can think of seeing these letters? Anything."

"I have no idea, what you mean. Could be anything he typed in. Could be a password to one of his accounts . . . Wi-fi, or anything."

"Yeah, similar things popped to my head, too, at first." Edgar kept holding the paper in front of her but didn't hand it over. "But if it's a password, pretty weak, I must say. No capitals, no numbers. I mean, I wrote 'em down here with capitals, but as you can see, caps lock and shift are clean. So are the numbers."

Lindsey was squirming on the sofa and a dew of sweat began to gloss on her forehead.

"Okay, I see, so you got any idea what it could be?" she asked. "And why is that so important after all?"

"Well, I spent some time scrambling these letters and—" Edgar stopped talking and turned the paper around in front of Lindsey.

WEETYIOSFHMM
MYWIFESHOTME

Lindsey's body temperature spiked sky high. She couldn't say a word.

"Might not be strong for a password, but it is for evidence."

"Look . . . I don't know—"

"Lindsey Louise Vaughn, you're under arrest for murder, attempted murder—"

"No, wait! Don't do this, it's a mistake! No—"

"And making false statements."

"No, it doesn't prove anything!! You can't do this!"

Lindsey's hysteria escalated by the second while Edgar read her rights in a mild manner, and Giordano, despite the intense fightback, adroitly laced her arms behind her back and clicked the shiny cuffs around her wrists.

Minutes after Edgar called for backup, a patrol car arrived.

"Ed," Giordano said with a smile after the officers drove away with Lindsey sobbing in the backseat.

"Hmm?"

"When we report to the major, just do everything like this, okay? Draw letters and shit. He's gonna love it."

Edgar released no comment on this. However, as a reward, he threw a wide smile, a smile so wide his partner had never seen one like it on his face before.

# Chapter 29

Edgar rarely moved at the tempo he was at as he cut through the office among desks and colleagues. His phone-occupied partner came close to spilling his coffee when he saw Edgar popping up from nowhere behind him.

"Excuse me, hold on a sec!" Giordano said into the receiver, motivated by his partner's "Hang up, it's really important" look.

"What?"

"Hayes woke up."

\*\*\*

Edgar and Giordano found themselves in a way more pleasant mood than they usually were when entering Major Rafferty's office.

"Good morning, boss."

"If you don't spoil it as usual, could be good," the major replied while pointing at the seats in front of his desk, which the two detectives then wordlessly occupied.

"Sadly, we won't spoil anything today."

"Alright, then. Could you speak with Hayes?"

"Yes. Though the guy's still a mess, he managed to recall and talk."

"Okay, let's hear it!"

"Well, one does not hear such a story every week."

\*\*\*

Edgar and Giordano had patiently waited until the nurse finished changing the infusion. She strictly instructed them to make it as short as possible, due to the critical nature of the period directly following awakening from a coma. Talking must not be forced.

The nurse left them alone so they could talk in private. Although words said in a hospital bed, especially under medication, wouldn't qualify as an official statement, the most important questions are often met with more satisfying answers than during a legitimate interrogation.

"Mr. Hayes," Edgar began. "First of all, we're very glad to see you awake. And to know . . . it seems you're likely gonna make it."

One of the corners of Sam's mouth morphed into a smile.

"And in the name of the entire police department, thank you for your trust."

Sam gave Edgar a puzzled look. Edgar continued.

"You could've just written it on the floor. Risking, of course, that your wife would spot it and erase it after your death. The keyboard, however, anticipating that any of us would notice, well . . . thank you."

A full-fledged smile sat on Sam's face. He clearly wasn't 100% yet, but he helpfully answered all their questions. At times, it was hard to understand him, but overall, he managed to provide enough to make the day for the detectives and their boss. Given his condition, he delivered pretty well-constructed answers and recalled a surprising number of details. The two detectives tried to make it short, as the nurse had instructed, but as Sam was unfolding the full story of that night, they both lost track of time.

"Why didn't you tell him your phone was in the other room?"

"That's what I just said. I was beginning to believe that he was telling the truth, but not enough to bet my phone and essentially my life on it."

Edgar nodded gently.

"And even if I believed that he came for my money, I still didn't know a hundred percent for sure that he wouldn't kill me because of some personal revenge or whatever after he got the money."

"Understand."

"No, you don't! More than once, I was on the verge of believing a second gunman did actually exist and might even still be in my house, but there was no evidence to support that. Right, there were signs, like the internet gone and shit, and the guy did sound honest, but—would you two have just believed it like that?"

The two detectives put their eyes down on the floor at almost the same time.

"But beyond that, let's say with time, I believed he wasn't the shooter. I still didn't want to tell him about the phone. If there was somebody hiding in there, and they hadn't spotted it yet, and I gave it away loud and clear . . ." Sam took a brief pause in his story, then continued. "But my clock was ticking, so if he didn't go to my car, sooner or later, I'd have to go for my phone. But it was more certain this way."

"Why didn't you get the phone sooner? I mean saying nothing, just sneaking around the room."

"Because of what I said. What if there was someone in there?"

"What do you mean more certain this way?" Giordano asked.

"Him getting out of the house seemed to confirm that no one was there. I figured the other one would never let him out." Sam paused for a moment. "Apparently I got that part wrong," he said with a little chuckle. "Anyway, it crossed my mind, of course, what if they are partners or something. But I saw that the most unlikely. And when I heard him already up there, I thought I gotta take the risk and let's see what we see."

Edgar and Giordano's eyes met for a second.

"Alright." Edgar nodded to acknowledge the story he'd just been told. "And why didn't your wife try to kill you before you called for help? What do you think? She had time. Why wait 'til you made the call?"

"Don't know . . . Maybe just . . . tried to be sure."

"Sure how?"

"If I call and say there is an armed man in my house who is trying kill me, that would've instantly crossed her off the suspects list. Ain't that right?"

Sam looked Edgar in the eye.

"Your wife—" Edgar stopped but continued shortly. "Why didn't you shoot her while you were fighting? If I'm understanding it right, you had the chance. And no doubt, it would've been rightful self-defense."

Sam bowed his head and remained in silence for a long moment.

"I knew I had much better chances in an investigation if none of us were dead," he answered right before Edgar could have apologized for the inconsiderate question.

He delivered his reply in a calm, emotionless tone. Although, it took some time for him to look in the detective's eyes again.

This question was never raised again.

*\*\**

167

"Does his wife know?" the major asked.

Giordano threw a delighted look at his partner, who was occupying a seat on his left.

"She burst out in tears of joy," Edgar replied.

Giordano chuckled and even the major released a fragment of a smile.

"Hayes's story pretty much put every piece in place—ski mask on the floor, car keys in Rowe's pocket. Even the safe confirms his version. I only wish we could hear the story from Rowe's perspective."

"The safe?"

Edgar looked at Giordano denoting that Giordano could carry on speaking. The young partner didn't hesitate.

"Its access log recorded that a wrong combination was entered twice. Time matches, all fits."

"Murdering her husband plus trying to take the money from the safe?" the major asked. "Why? She's the wife, no kids. Wouldn't she have benefited anyway if the man kicked the bucket?"

"We have asked this very question too," Giordano said.

"And what sort of answer we giving to that?" the major asked.

Edgar delivered the answer. "Perhaps she tried to make it look like a robbery, hoping it'd drive the police's attention away from the people close to him."

"If the victim lies next to an intact door and safe, both wide open . . . we may not rule out people close to him once and for all," the major said with a bit of sarcasm. "Or am I wrong?"

"I'm only saying, this is what she probably thought we'd be thinking. Don't matter if there are signs of forced entry or not. Stranger or relative, both could surprise him outside the house and make him cooperate before killing him. But if there's money missing from the safe, it's true, the wife wouldn't be the first one to look at closely. Of course, as one of the prime beneficiaries of the tragedy, she isn't above all suspicion, but . . . as a point in her defense, would have been pretty solid."

"Smart."

"Thank you, boss!" Edgar replied appreciatively.

"Not you, the slut. It's part of your job."

Giordano's chuckle got put out by Edgar's look of disapproval.

"Wouldn't have been any problem, even with her little trick blown by the wrong combination," Edgar continued. "But . . . on her way out, she probably bumped into the other uninvited guest."

The major stewed on all this for a moment. Steep but fundamentally coherent story, it seemed. Even if not in every detail.

"How does he know she was messing with the safe? He wasn't conscious. Or was he?"

"No, Rowe told him after they discovered his wife was the shooter. He said he heard some beeping sound coming from that room when he entered the house. He just didn't know what it was then."

"So, it's based on what the dead guy said to the other guy who just woke up from coma?"

"He wasn't particularly dead then."

Lucky for Giordano, the major didn't have time to award this comment. Edgar immediately jumped in and saved the day.

"History books ain't quite filled with stories of the living either."

"Yeah, right," the major said. "But still, both of them just happened to trespass at the very same time? What are the odds?"

"You didn't see *National Treasure*?" Giordano asked, hoping once again to roll the hard six. But the looks his superiors rolled on him made Giordano come down instantly and begin with an explanation. "Don't worry, I won't spoil anything, sirs."

Giordano paused, but the major nodded for him to continue, so he did.

"So, two gangs, no sharing of plans, choosing the very same evening to break into a certain place because they both know that's the time when they got the best chance of succeeding."

Edgar and the major glanced at each other and seemed to be in agreement that the young detective's movie reference actually made a decent amount of sense.

"She could very well be aware of her husband's schedule and know his whereabouts," Giordano said. "The other guy, well, he might have been tailing him for weeks, so . . ."

Giordano's superiors seemed to appreciate the interesting parallel. Edgar took up the story.

"Hayes said he didn't believe him partly because it sounded absurd. But then, he also said that before he got shot, he spent like an hour talking online with one of his friends. Right after he came home. The exact time of her arrival is unclear. She might have waited for him somewhere. And probably, if it wasn't for that video call, she wouldn't have hung around that long. Seems obvious, she didn't want to take the shot while he's in live chat with someone."

"Okay, so let's say they arrived roughly within an hour of each other. Doesn't sound much more plausible."

"Not much," Edgar agreed. "A bit, though . . . We might find out if she decides to confess."

"Huh!" Giordano chuckled suddenly.

"What's so funny, son?" the major asked after failing to hear any kind of words following the sound that had erupted from the young colleague.

"If I think about it, all it would've taken was Hayes weeding out some hair when he ripped off the mask from his wife's head."

The major gave a grumpy look to Giordano, just to not break the habit. Yet, he appreciated that this time the young detective's joy was fueled by a reasonable thought, not another movie comparison.

*If you lose your hair, you won't be the heir.* Edgar suffered a minor shock when this lame joke was born in his head. He deemed it beyond debate that it was a repercussion of his time spent with his partner. But since he kept it to himself, he didn't hold him accountable. Rather, he began with the next topic.

"It doesn't matter anymore. Although, there is something else. We didn't mention it last time."

"What?" the major asked.

"We believe she had an accomplice," Edgar answered.

"Out there?"

"No. But there might have been someone who . . . maybe waited somewhere to pick her up, to provide an alibi, or something."

"What makes you think that?"

"Her phone," Giordano replied before Edgar, who didn't seem to mind.

"What about it?"

"She had an old LG on her that night," Edgar answered, as he and his partner smoothly took turns replying to the major's questions. "We saw it in the hospital the day after. Seemed odd so we asked her about it, and she casually admitted it's a second cell phone."

"I just enjoy staying away from smart phones," Giordano added. "Quote, unquote."

"Is that it?

"No," Edgar answered. "She called someone from the ambulance. Openly, out-loud. And she seemed more than comfortable to identify that person."

"Right. Tell me about this person."

"Elizabeth Viola Rantzen," Edgar said. "Friend from school, ex-colleague, currently a store manager. Nothing special. She was, indeed, the person who received that call. She even showed us the call list in her phone."

"Her legitimate phone," Giordano added.

"That night she was home alone, apparently," Edgar continued. "She ordered pizza to her address, and the delivery guy confirmed that she opened the door. She tipped quite big, he said. But it was very late, long after the hillside party had wrapped up."

"So no alibi," the major said.

"Nope," Edgar replied. "But given how this case is, you might ask: why would she need one. Question is: did she know about her friend's actions or even contribute somehow. Providing the gun, whatever. And so far no signs of her having been involved in any way, shape or form."

"When we talked to her, she seemed a bit nervous but that's all," Giordano added.

"So maybe it's a dead end," the major said.

"Yes, it could be," Edgar said. "She might enjoy staying away from smart phones sometimes. Say it's true. But honestly, why would she have any kinds of phone on her while attempting to kill her husband? To be in touch with someone? Like who?"

"Okay," the major said. "Did you ask the wife to give that phone over, at any point?"

172

Edgar and Giordano looked at each other.

"We thought about it," Giordano began, "but—"

"But what?" the major asked, urging the rest of the answer since Giordano seemed to be hesitant to deliver it.

"She didn't destroy it, didn't even try to hide it," Edgar said, helping his partner out. "And overall she appeared to be way too open about it."

"We figured even if this Elizabeth was involved some way, they'd probably been smart enough not to incriminate themselves," Giordano added. "So even if we extracted records from the phone company, we'd likely find nothing."

"It's either the wife made that call just to play the blameless victim, and the clueless friend received it horrified. Or it was a coded warning call to the silent partner."

Giordano nodded on Edgar's spot on summarization.

"Point is," Edgar continued. "Hayes's cunning message essentially put his wife behind bars already. And he even gave us the courtesy of waking up, so . . . should be all good. How much she gets for Rowe, that's another thing because no matter how we slice it, he was an armed intruder. But that's not up to us."

"But the accomplice thread, we'll follow up," Giordano added with a serious face.

"Alright," the major said after a short silence. "Okay boys, good job . . . Maybe no one will be demoted today."

The officers spent a few more minutes talking in a light-hearted, casual manner. At least two of them. Edgar believed that, even if there was no accomplice and the court order would be appropriate, the case would still not be concluded. Might be closed officially, but it wouldn't be over.

# Chapter 30

"It's all because of me."

Edgar struggled with how to respond to the girl's statement. Despite all his efforts, there was a huge delay before he spoke.

"No," he finally said. "I mean . . . No! It's not your fault, don't even think—"

"I didn't say it's my fault." Cynthia's voice was cracking. "But it happened because of me."

Edgar was in terrible trouble. Here was this lovely, young lady who was stuck between two wheels that she might never be rid of. Cynthia's mother had passed away a few years ago, and less than a week ago, Cynthia's father had joined her. The only thing one could and should do now was to dispel her guilt completely.

But Edgar had no idea how to proceed. Of course it had all happened because of her. Lying would be utterly pointless. Making Cynthia believe in Santa wouldn't be nearly as hard as convincing her that she was not the one and only motivation for her father to approach that house with a gun in his hand.

Cynthia started weeping again. Edgar composed himself.

"What your father was going to do and what he did is, no doubt, illegal and questionable. But he did it as a father. Of course, this word doesn't justify everything. But so many words out there are being abused by people every day. Wish it was the only one." Edgar saw that her teary eyes were paying full attention to him, so he continued with more confidence. "Once, I abused my position in the police force because of my daughter. She had a very important school dance. She had been training the whole year. And due to work, I completely lost track of the days." Edgar paused here then continued in a slightly more melancholic tone. "At least . . . that's what I told them when they asked why I showed up at the last minute. Just in time, but at the very last minute. Fact is, I totally forgot. The night before, after work, we went out with the guys for a few beers, and I never got home until morning. I woke up in the afternoon and only one slip of paper was there to remind me. My daughter's message on the fridge."

Cynthia was listening attentively to Edgar's story. As was Giordano, despite having heard it already. Usually he is not opposed to speak without being spoken to, but this time he just sat next to his partner saying nothing.

"My driving and flashing lights made like a dozen drivers run up on the curb. I almost caused an accident twice—at least. It's a wonder no one reported it." Edgar started to brood but stopped himself. He knew it was not the right time for such a thing. He had a job to do now. "It took me a long while to tell my daughter what really happened. But when I did, her eyes told me that I was hurting her feelings. But . . . they also told me that . . . she thought no less of me. Even though, I would've deserved that."

The streams of tears on Cynthia's face began to run dry. Edgar didn't really know where he was going with this, but he wanted to keep talking, anything that could possibly bring relief to Cynthia's pain.

Unbeknownst to Edgar, Jessica was standing still and quiet in the doorway, listening to Edgar's story the whole time. She was moved by the detective's words and appreciated how Edgar was focusing all his attention on trying to console Cynthia.

"I couldn't take one sip in the next two months," Edgar continued.

Giordano unintentionally released a tiny smile as he thought about how those sips had ceased a while ago and also how his partner was opening up to this girl. He watched the two them talking, and it felt like a vulnerable soul trying to heal a broken one.

"If I'd been in your dad's position and doing what he did," Edgar said, "I'd never have told my girl . . . but I wouldn't have felt ashamed—not for one minute."

Cynthia sighed deeply, and the three grown-ups waited for her reaction, as if it had been rehearsed.

"So . . . you sure he didn't want to hurt that man?" Cynthia asked.

"Damn sure! Confirmed by the man's own words," Edgar replied. "They didn't know each other in person and had nothing to do with one another. At least, we found no trace of it. Most likely, your dad heard about the man and his business reputation. We don't really know from who or how, but the point is, he could've learned a few things from someone, might even have done some research, and decided to try to . . . take some money from him by force. He probably thought that whatever he took, that man wouldn't suffer much from it. And looking at his business interests, properties, and other stuff, he likely got that part right. The guy is a real fat cat and likes playing dodgy, so . . ." Edgar leaned closer to the girl. "I'm saying it just to you . . . and not as a policeman . . . If there's someone between your dad and me who deserves to be despised by his own daughter, that's certainly not your old man."

Cynthia failed to hold her tears. The streams gained thickness again; she was unable to talk. Edgar softly held her hand, and she clasped his tightly in return. Jessica turned toward the kitchen because she couldn't take more.

Edgar and Giordano said goodbye to Cynthia then exchanged a few more words with Jessica out on the porch.

"You know how much you'll get after Austin?" Edgar asked as politely as he could.

"She will be getting something as an orphan and some other allowances," Jessica replied. "Gonna be enough for living, but . . . nothing else. Definitely nothing else."

\*\*\*

The visit to Austin's family was the last of Edgar's duties for the day. Yet, he didn't make it home for another two hours at least. He dropped Giordano off at his condo and kept on driving. After a while, he stopped at a park and sat himself on a bench.

This case had him very stirred up. Not as a professional, as it would extend the line of his solved cases, after all. But emotionally, Edgar had never been so invested in a case— ever. He knew he had to push this aside and divert his focus back to the professional angle, given there was still some work left to do, like shedding light on the possible accomplice. But despite how hard he tried, he only managed to get a small fraction of his thoughts to work on accomplishing that. The vast majority of his brain was searching for a solution to a problem of an entirely different nature. A problem that was closely connected to the case, but if it were solved, it would certainly not end up on the pages of the official files.

# Chapter 31

"So, Vaughn finally spat out her confession," the major said.

"Yep, and what a confession that is," Giordano added.

Giordano and Edgar were occupying their regular seats in Major Rafferty's office.

"Make it short. I want to read the whole report."

"Well, in short, she confessed everything."

"Excellent."

"Yes," Edgar acknowledged. "Kinda scary, though, how not a single bit of it contradicts Hayes's story."

"Is that so?"

"Nowhere is there a detail or a part where she tries to salvage something by throwing some bullshit defense. Nothing. As a matter of fact, I've never seen anything like this in my life."

The major nodded contentedly before continuing with further questions. "So why did she do it?"

"Personal reasons. Refused to elaborate," Edgar said.

"Right. What about the accomplice part?"

"Nothing," Giordano replied.

"Nothing?"

Edgar shook his head.

"You mean she didn't involve anyone in her confession? Not even that Elizabeth you were looking at?"

"No," Giordano said.

"We believe her?"

"Haven't decided yet," Edgar answered.

"Okay. Let's think like her . . . She confesses everything. Facing several years. But she's got a partner she could offer up as part of a deal. Yet, she doesn't?"

"Agree," Edgar said. "Hard to imagine this woman defending someone at the expense of her own years. To be honest, it made us unsure."

"So, what is the basis of your accomplice theory? Nothing but her second cell phone? That's it?"

"Yes," Giordano answered without hesitation.

"What about the search at Elizabeth's?"

"Nothing, she's clean," Giordano said. "Same with the phone records. As we said before, they must have been cautious enough to leave no evidence."

"So we drop it?" the major asked.

"Hold on," Edgar said. "We didn't let go and kept digging. And we found something interesting."

"I'm listening."

"All right. Let alone Vaughn and her personal reasons for a moment. Is there anyone else whose best interest might have been served by her success?"

"Could be plenty of 'em out there interested in Hayes crossing the river," the major said.

"That's right," Edgar agreed. "But not all of them maintain direct contact with the one who tried to murder him."

The major leaned forward in his chair.

"Elizabeth Rantzen, on her own, appears to be above suspicion. But her husband is . . . uh, the fuck's his name?" Edgar turned to his partner.

"Roland Elliot Dunkley," Giordano replied.

"Who the hell is that?"

"A heavyweight mogul," Edgar said. "Among other things, he's the CEO of the telecom company that's the biggest competitor to Hayes's."

"Hm, promising. Except, not really . . . If Vaughn's got three other top dogs as super close friends, then what? That doesn't mean all of them were involved—Wait!" The major interrupted himself. "Did you ask Hayes about this?"

"Here comes the point," Edgar said. "We saw him only once since then and not too long."

"He wasn't in his best form," Giordano added. "Even more heavily medicated than the first time we spoke to him."

"His full recovery's going to take some more time. But to the question of could she be assisted by someone or someones—"

"He said the same name." The major stole the concluding part of Edgar's sentence.

"Exactly," Edgar confirmed. "Although, this still could be a dead end. Even though Rantzen's alibi is somewhat questionable, there's still no evidence of her involvement. Dunkley, even better. He was on a business trip, wasn't even in the state."

"For me, he knew nothing about this," Giordano added quietly.

"Never pleases me hearing my men talking about dead ends," the major said.

"You called it that first," Giordano replied with a little smile, referring to their previous briefing.

"Wait," the major said. "If Dunkley had no idea about any of this, why you involving him at all?"

Edgar and Giordano turned to each other in such an identical way and pace, it was as if they had trained for it.

"You tell the best part or shall I?" Edgar asked his partner courteously.

"Please, go ahead."

"Those supposed personal reasons. Could be anything. Jealousy, right? Probably Hayes had affairs, but doubt that's all it was, Major."

"What then?"

"If, say, Hayes wanted to divorce. That would've been pretty bad for Vaughn."

"How bad could it be?" the major asked. "I mean, I'm no expert of divorce settlements and such, thank God, but they've been married for years for God's sake!"

"Yes, they're married, but we dug deeper and turned out that due to the inheritance succession, his assets would mostly have passed to the relatives. Brother, mother, and few other close ones. But absent the will, it's pretty hard to see through what would have passed to whom exactly. In this case, the poor widow would've made some fortune, yes, but no jackpot, for sure."

"I see . . . Nice."

"But, if Hayes was gone," Edgar went on explaining the situation, "the whole of his company lands in the hands of his brother, Kevin. Who is less than motivated to take care of that and even reputed to be dumb about business, so he'd certainly sell it to the first bidder. Probably way underpriced."

"Tell me more about this, especially the first bidder part."

"Yep . . . uh, these are just rumors. Smear campaign and shit."

"These are the kind of sources we build on lately?"

"No, but if we don't know exactly what to look for, we gotta turn every rock."

"Right, go on."

"So, with the little brother in charge Dunkley would certainly seize the opportunity to finally get his hands on Hayes's company. In other words, if the husband of Vaughn's big friend merges the two companies into one, thus hitting the ultimate jackpot, then maybe the person who made it all possible, who also happens to be a good friend of the family, would come out very well too.

"This is how Dunkley is involved," Giordano said. "He might have known nothing, but, potentially, he'd have benefitted the most. And the ones close to him."

"Guys, guys! You telling me . . ."

"She did it." Edgar took over the sentence after the major stopped. "But maybe it wasn't her idea. Maybe she just approved and agreed to do the dirty work."

"Oh, Jesus!" The major was astounded. "I should have retired a long time ago."

Inserting a joke here would have been the most obvious thing in the world. Yet, both detectives remained silent.

"But if that's true and Rantzen isn't just a partner in crime, but the originator, basically" the major said, "then why the hell would Vaughn take all the credits for herself?"

"We admit this part is a real head-scratcher," Giordano said. "But maybe she thinks protecting the friend with the influential husband who's got good connections could somehow benefit her in the process. Who knows?"

"We're trying to get to the bottom of it, boss," Edgar added. "But the thing is, if all it was, was that two or more people discussed it in a room somewhere, but there was no actual act of assistance, like picking her up or providing an alibi, and Vaughn won't turn anyone in—"

"Or due to lack of evidence, she couldn't even if she wanted to," Giordano added.

"—then there's not much we can do." Edgar delivered the punch line.

# Chapter 32

"Robin Wright," Giordano stated firmly.

"What about her?"

"That lady from Evidence Control. I've been thinking about her since then. Who does she look like?"

"Great. I see now why you were such a big help throughout this."

"Hey!"

Edgar freed a small but rather evil smirk. "In the end, you've taken a liking to the morgue after all?"

"Maybe."

"She's too old for you."

"She's past 60?" Giordano asked.

"Nope."

"Then what the hell you talking about?"

The proportions of Edgar's smile shifted—less evil but bigger.

The two detectives were walking back to their car from a roadside diner, munching the last bites of their sandwiches and slurping their soda cups dry.

"Listen, uh, I gotta tell you something," Edgar said before they hopped in.

"Go on."

Edgar briefly explained the conclusion he had come to lately and the idea that had nested itself in his head. Giordano was anything but fascinated and didn't shy away from going vocal.

"And what is your plan exactly? Go visit him in the hospital, towering over his bed and threatening him with your scowling eyebrows?"

"Who said threatening?"

"Then?"

"A bit of leverage will do just fine. No eyebrows required."

"Really? I'm reluctant to lecture you, but we ain't working for the IRS," Giordano said, still unconvinced.

"I'm aware of that."

"And we're not even financial crime detectives," Giordano continued. "They tried to rob him, his own wife nearly killed him, and you wanna tell him that we just now happened to slide into the mood to investigate his financials? I have no doubt the guy's dirty, but still, that would be kinda dickish. Even from the police. Like if a speeder wraps themself around a tree, we click the cuffs on first, then let 'em have a medic. Not saying it's undeserved, but—"

"Cut the preach, I get what you mean," Edgar said while ripping open the car door. "Get in!"

Giordano did as he was told.

"Just a discrete conversation." Edgar added as he turned the ignition key.

"And what would you say to him? I mean specifically."

"Like, currently no one is intending to conduct any investigation related to his business life and . . . guess, it would be preferrable to keep it that way. Or something like that."

The determination on Edgar's face was accompanied by a level of hesitancy that Giordano had never seen before on his partner.

"Look," Edgar said, "I don't know how he's dealing with his murderous wifey, mentally and emotionally, and to be frank, I don't really care. But the dude just barely managed to cheat death."

"So?"

"So, I'm not saying it's gonna make him find God or something, but maybe it's just enough for him not to give two shits about the money the poor bastard tried to take from him for his daughter."

It clearly got Giordano thinking.

"You remember what you said about the view of dead bodies?" Edgar asked. "Which one's killing you more, seeing them at the crime scene or in the morgue."

"Wasn't that long ago. I remember."

"You want to know what's the part that really kills me? Young victims. Wherever they are. I fully understand what you're saying and all, but . . ." Edgar's words stopped coming for a moment, then he continued. "I'd rather see an eighty-year-old on a steel tray than an eighteen-year-old in a wheelchair."

"Cynthia isn't a victim, though . . . I get what you mean, hell I do, just . . ."

Edgar looked at his partner. "Not a crime victim."

Giordano was silent for a while before he spoke. "The wheelchair isn't your biggest concern about her, but what we discussed after we left them. Right?"

"If I say yes, you start arguing, right?"

"They had the funeral a few days ago. According to Austin's girlfriend, she seems to be getting a little better, and she didn't turn down the psychologist they appointed her either. That look like giving up to you? Plus, that little speech you gave her . . ."

Edgar didn't interrupt.

"But hell, don't think I'm against you, Ed. I just don't see how it could possibly work out."

"I'll figure it out."

"Alright. You're the boss . . . Worth a shot."

Edgar nodded.

"So . . . when you wanna visit?"

"I don't know. I'll sleep on it. Why?"

"I'll help you."

"You don't have to. Not in this."

"Why?"

"Because it's sadly outside our detective boundaries."

"Further outside than using police lights to get to a dance gig?"

Edgar's smile was no more than a six out of ten, at best. "You see? You can tell that to Hayes," he said.

"What?"

"I don't mind taking extreme measures."

Giordano, of course, delivered his regular smile as a comment on Edgar's proposition. "But actually . . . we could work with this," he said.

"With what?"

"The girl. I mean, just to mention, what we were talking about in the car . . . instead of blackmail."

"No. We won't need any of them."

# Chapter 33

At first, Sam couldn't believe his ears. He knew he wasn't dreaming, and he knew he wasn't medicated enough to hallucinate such a thing. So, he had no choice but to absorb and accept what he had just heard. He found the idea itself appalling enough, and the obscene timing made it even worse. But the detectives quickly made him understand that there had never been a more appropriate occasion to practice self-control, however justified an emotional outburst might be. Words were traded between Sam and Edgar, while Giordano stood by the door, silently and dispassionately observing the other two.

"This is blackmail, gentlemen."

"Not at all. Just a proposition. Although what we call it also depends on the tone and manner we choose to discuss it in."

*What fancy-ass talk. From a chump cop.*

"Look, we don't intend to blackmail or threaten you, not by any means." Edgar raised his voice a bit. "We're aware that what we're talking about now isn't entirely right. Still, I recommend you consider it."

Sam was already opening his mouth to interrupt, but Edgar kept going without losing momentum.

"Yes, us two are only interested in the armed attack that happened in your house. Regarding which you have nothing to worry about, apparently. But you might, regarding other things."

Sam's face didn't particularly suggest he was inclined to consent.

"You offended by the timing? Please, if you wish, we're more than happy to wait until they remove the stitches and let you go, and only after that, we tell the guys at the Financial Crimes Division to start looking at you more closely."

Giordano did a stellar job of keeping his face emotionless, totally hiding his astonishment about his partner's raw style.

"But to tell you the truth, that's not what we want . . . Listen, you get along in life the way you do. I'm not saying you should feel sorry for the poor devil who wanted to rob you. Or for his family, who you never met. But if there's a perfect chance for one to give something back, then this is it."

Sam gulped. "Even if there are some people out there who I should give something back to, he ain't one of them. And neither is his daughter."

"I know."

"I am sorry for the little girl. I truly am. But not my problem. I don't owe them a damn thing."

"No, you don't. Unlike your wife. Who's not likely to be able to pay."

"She didn't shoot him on the street! Or in his own home. I don't wanna defend Lindsey, believe me, but your guy wasn't supposed to be there."

"He wasn't, indeed. But no matter which way we cut it, you have a lot to thank him for. Even if it's all not exactly what he intended."

"What? What the hell you mean? If he didn't show up in my house, my wife would've been gone and I could've called for help right after I woke up. He is actually the very reason I almost checked out."

"Maybe. But he's also the very reason your wife got busted."

Sam didn't argue the point.

"We would've been looking with enormous forces, rest assured, but I gotta say, she planned it all out quite well. We may not have been able to catch her. What do you think, how long would you have been safe around her?"

Sam still didn't show signs of wanting to argue.

"Look, obviously, you're the only one out of the three who didn't commit a crime there that night. Them two, yes, and they're paying the price. But for how many crimes should you pay the price?"

"Is this really the tone and manner you wanna choose?"

"Listen, I told you, I don't wanna threaten you."

"You just did, pal."

"Right. And you know what? I take it back."

"Sure you do."

"You have my word."

Giordano began struggling to maintain his poker face. Lucky for him, it didn't really matter since no one in the room was paying attention to him.

"If you get out of here and pick up right where you left off, sooner or later, you'll break your neck anyway, you won't need our help."

"Then nothing to worry about."

"But don't forget, someone else died instead of you that night. Doesn't matter the reason he went there. If it wasn't for him, that wouldn't have been your wife's only chance to get what she wanted. Maybe now, she'd be counting the assets she's about to receive after you, and not the years behind bars . . . You know, this isn't my first time talking to a heartless, unscrupulous, douchebag."

Edgar's unvarnished honesty met with Sam's appreciative smile.

"But you are the first one I believe every word of."

Sam turned serious.

"And if I'm being honest," Edgar said. "I don't like what you're saying. Nor what I am saying. So, I think we're pretty much done here. We won't bother you any longer. We walk out of that door right now and what we discussed will never come up ever again. You have my word. But before we go, one more thing."

Sam couldn't help but be curious.

"According to your statement, you offered him money. More than once. The last time, lying behind the sofa with two bullets in your body. You told him that if he helped, and you made it, he'd get the money he needs . . . Now, you might not have gotten to sealing the deal, but . . . one way or another, Austin Rowe did stick to his part. And his death changes nothing. So I'm asking you, as a businessman—you willing to stick to your part?"

Following a short contemplation, Sam answered. "Like you said, we never got to seal the deal. And he didn't help me or whatnot. He just kept Lindsey occupied for a while. Which I used to my advantage."

Edgar's blood pressure began to rise. He slowly turned to his partner and reached out his hand.

"Your phone."

Giordano didn't seem to get it at first. But that changed before Edgar had to ask again.

All Edgar had to do was to give the phone to Sam, since Giordano had already unlocked it with a password and selected the image.

"Not the most well-composed message. But says enough."

Sam looked at the message. The one written by his former "guest" prior to his death. The part he wrote about him.

*He is a rich man and ~~crooked~~ Convince him to help my little girl. He can afford and if you ask him I am sure he will listen to you.*

The word "crooked" was crossed out so many times, it was hardly readable.

Sam stared ahead, silent. Giordano's cell phone was still in his hand but the screen already went dark.

Edgar figured he had said and done everything he could. Now it was time to wait without words.

After a long silence, Sam looked up at Edgar and declared his final opinion about this proposition.

"You would have saved time by starting with this."

End